Polyester
The Musical

Book by
Phil Olson

Music by
Wayland Pickard

Lyrics by
Phil Olson & Wayland Pickard

A SAMUEL FRENCH ACTING EDITION

SAMUEL
FRENCH
FOUNDED 1830
NEW YORK HOLLYWOOD LONDON TORONTO

SAMUELFRENCH.COM

ISBN 978-0-573-69827-9   Printed in U.S.A.   #29289

RENTAL MATERIALS

An orchestration consisting of a **Piano/Vocal Score**, **Rehearsal CD** and **Performance CD** will be loaned two months prior to the production ONLY on the receipt of the Licensing Fee quoted for all performances, the rental fee and a refundable deposit.

Please contact Samuel French for perusal of the music materials as well as a performance license application.

IMPORTANT BILLING AND CREDIT REQUIREMENTS

All producers of *POLYESTER must* give credit to the Author of the Play in all programs distributed in connection with performances of the Play, and in all instances in which the title of the Play appears for the purposes of advertising, publicizing or otherwise exploiting the Play and/or a production. The name of the Author *must* appear on a separate line on which no other name appears, immediately following the title and *must* appear in size of type not less than fifty percent of the size of the title type.

In addition the following credit *must* be given in all programs and publicity information distributed in association with this piece:

POLYESTER THE MUSICAL

Book by	Music by
Phil Olson	**Wayland Pickard**

Lyrics by
Phil Olson & Wayland Pickard

POLYESTER was first produced at Actors Forum Theatre in Los Angeles, California, in November 2009. It was directed by Wayland Pickard and Doug Engalla, the choreography was by Michele Bernath, the producer was DHM Entertainment, the associate producer was Laura Coker, the orchestrations, arrangements and sound design were by Wayland Pickard, and the lighting design was by Carey Dunn. The cast, in order of appearance, was as follows:

LANCE. . . . . Robert Moon
MINDY. . . . . Pamela Donnelly
BARRY. . . . . Christopher Fairbanks
CARL. . . . . Jim Staahl
PEGGY. . . . . Gwendolyn Druyor

CHARACTERS

LANCE – Hyper, overly enthusiastic fan of The Synchronistics and host of the WKLN TV telethon. The local weatherman.

CARL – Not the brightest bulb in the box. He's had a little too much hippie lettuce in the past.

PEGGY – Wholesome, shy. Just slightly smarter than Carl. Performs in the shadow of Mindy.

BARRY – Mindy's ex-husband. Cheated on her which led to the group's break-up. Wrote most of their songs, including their most famous, "*Better Together.*" Not very self-aware.

MINDY – The Stevie Nicks figurehead of the group. Scorned and bitter from Barry's affair.

ACT I

SCENE 1: The 1999 WKLN Public Access TV Station Telethon, at the WKLN Studio in Maple Valley.

"Together as Friends" ....Ensemble

"A Howard Johnson's in Green Bay" ....Mindy & Ensemble

"I Want You, But I Hurt You" ....Barry & Ensemble

"I Watch You Cause I Love You".......................Carl & Peggy

"No More Men"...................................Mindy & Peggy

"My Little Man-Child" ....Peggy

"The Funk Train".......................................Ensemble

"Remember The Good Times We Had"...................Ensemble

ACT II

SCENE 1: Same place, 15 minutes later.

"Synchronistic Dancin'".............................Ensemble

"Bump Your Booty Rump" ....Ensemble

"Tough Love"..Ensemble

"You Yank My Chain"................................Ensemble

"The War on Love" ....Carl

"Run Groundhog Run".....................................Peggy

"Mindy's Song"................................. Barry & Mindy

"Better Together".....................................Ensemble

Medley – Reprise ....Ensemble

ACT I

(Downstage center are four microphones on stands. On the back wall is a sign that reads, "Maple Valley and the 1999 WKLN TV Telethon Welcome The Synchronistics." Downstage right is an "On Air" sign. It's not lit up. Downstage left is a huge poster of some sort, on an easel. Hanging over the "poster" is a black sheet that conceals what it is. Centerstage left is a small table with bottles of water on it. There's a stool upstage of the table against the wall, and another stool downstage of the table. Stage right against the wall are two more stools.)

LANCE. *(offstage, into the microphone, in an "NPR" voice)* And that concludes the farm report on WKLN TV, your public access partner in Maple Valley.

WKLN SINGERS. *(offstage) (sung by* **BARRY, MINDY, PEGGY & CARL***)*

WKLN. MAPLE VAL-LEY.

LANCE. *(offstage)* Today's regularly scheduled city council meeting will not be seen, thank goodness, in order to present the 1999 WKLN TV Telethon in its entirety, hosted by Maple Valley's very own Lance Chadwick.

(He enters the stage, still talking into the mic, using his "NPR" voice. As he talks, he walks downstage left to the "poster.")

That's Lance Chadwick, celebrity, humanitarian, handsome and articulate award-deserving weatherman for Channel 9. Lance is available for birthdays, weddings and bar mitzvahs. And now, Lance Chadwick.

(During the Station Manager's countdown, he takes the black sheet off the "poster," revealing what it is, a huge working, telethon pledge thermometer. He tosses the

black sheet offstage. Currently, the thermometer is set at "zero." Written at the top of the thermometer is, "Goal $10,000." At the bottom it reads, "WKLN says, 'Pledge like there's no tomorrow!'")

STATION MANAGER. *(V.O.)* And we're live in five...four... three, two...one.

(The "On Air" light turns on.)

LANCE. *(with a big fake smile, looking straight ahead at the "camera", in his "weatherman" voice)* I'm Lance Chadwick. You may recognize me from doing the weather on Channel 9, well the forecast today is partly rowdy with a chance of mirth...

(gives a big smile)

...because today we have a special treat for you.

(excited, losing it a little)

Oh, my gosh, this is so exciting, I can't believe it.

(takes a deep breath)

Today we have a group that got their first break right here, twenty years ago on WKLN TV, and, oh, my gosh...

(composing himself)

They're here today to help us reach our goal of ten thousand dollars, so we can continue to bring you quality programming such as the science fair special,

(reading the note card)

"Physical Parameters of Inorganic Compounds Found in Zirconium."

(He reacts to the absurd title. The music starts.)

And now, ladies and gentlemen, best known for their hit single "Better Together" which rose to number two on the Billboard charts, booked to be on Johnny Carson but they never showed up. "The Synchronistics!"

*(One by one, **MINDY**, **BARRY**, **CARL** and **PEGGY** come out of different doors, singing, wearing colorful polyester*

ABBA type outfits from the 70s. It's obvious that they're seeing each other for the first time in 20 years. **MINDY** *and* **BARRY** *are putting on their best faces, but they are clearly upset at each other.* **PEGGY** *is aware of the tension.* **CARL** *is oblivious. They line up in front of the four microphones. At the far stage right mic is* **CARL,** *then* **PEGGY,** *then* **MINDY,** *then* **BARRY.**)

CARL & PEGGY & BARRY & MINDY. *(singing)*
> SHA LA LA LA, LA LA LA LA LA
> SHA LA LA LA, LA LA LA LA
> SHA LA LA LA, LA LA LA LA LA
> SHA LA LA LA, LA LA LA LA
> WE'RE TOGETHER AS FRIENDS, SINGIN' IN HARMONY.

BARRY.
> ALL TOGETHER, SINGIN' ALL TOGETHER.

CARL & PEGGY & BARRY & MINDY.
> THE FOUR OF US IN SYNCHRONICITY.

BARRY.
> ALL TOGETHER, FRIENDS WE'LL BE FOREVER.

BARRY & CARL.	**MINDY & PEGGY.**
ANYTHING IS POSSIBLE.	OOOOOOH.

BARRY & CARL.	**MINDY & PEGGY.**
SET YOUR WORRIES	OOOOOOH.
FREE.	AAAAAH.

CARL & PEGGY & BARRY & MINDY.
> WHEN YOU'RE SINGIN' IN HARMONY.
> ALL TOGETHER. ALL FOUR TOGETHER.
> ALL TOGETHER, IN HOT OR COLD WEATHER.

BARRY & PEGGY.
> BIRDS OF A FEATHER.

CARL.
> WE WHAT?

BARRY & PEGGY.
> WE FLOCK TOGETHER.

CARL & PEGGY & BARRY & MINDY.
> FLOCK TOGETHER NOW!

CARL. Ladies and Gentlemen, it's great to be back in…

(Forgetting where he is, he looks back at the Maple Valley sign.)

Maple Valley. It's been a long dry spell. Hopefully we can redeem ourselves and make ten thousand dollars so the station won't fade into obscurity like we did.

CARL & PEGGY & BARRY & MINDY.

WHEN YOU'RE TOGETHER AS FRIENDS, SINGIN' IN HARMO…

BARRY & CARL.	**PEGGY & MINDY.**
NY…	…YOUR DREAMS WILL ASCEND, SINGIN' IN HARMO…

BARRY & CARL.	**PEGGY & MINDY.**
…THE LOVE NEVER ENDS,	NY…

CARL & PEGGY & BARRY & MINDY.

SINGIN' IN HARMONY.
HARMONY!

(The four of them stay at their mics. The tension between **BARRY** *and* **MINDY** *continues.)*

LANCE. *(applauding enthusiastically)* Oh, my gosh! Pinch me! Wow! This is just so amazing. This group right here, The Synchronistics, was a semi-finalist in the American Bandstand preliminaries, and they're here today to help raise money for WKLN so we can continue to bring you quality programming such as,

(reading from the note card)

"Income Tax Basics and the Importance of Reconciling Form 941. Schedule C."

(Looks offstage re: the title, then back to the camera.)

Our operator is ready, so pick up the phone and dial 516-WKLN with your generous pledge. She's waiting for your call…

(He looks over to the phone operator, Erma, who is offstage left. We can't see Erma. He looks back to the camera.)

Her name is Erma. Erma just turned 80.

(He looks over to Erma, yelling:)

LANCE. *(cont.)* Happy birthday, Erma! I like your new walker! It's got a horn!

(We hear a bicycle horn sound effect.)

Nice. Any pledges, yet?…Nothing?

(back to the camera)

Okay, let's go ahead and introduce the group, and find out what they've been up to for the past twenty years. This is awesome. Who's first?

(LANCE looks at the group. CARL looks at the others, then steps up to his mic.)

CARL. Okay, umm, I'm Carl. Namaste.

(He bows with prayer hands.)

I live with my mom. And I work at the syrup factory.

LANCE. Fantastic.

PEGGY. *(leaning into the mic, shy)* Umm, I'm Peggy. I teach driver's training, and I'm learning to speak Canadian.

LANCE. I'll have a beer, eh?

(He laughs.)

That's Canadian.

BARRY. *(into the mic)* I'm Barry. Thank you. I…

LANCE. *(interrupts BARRY)* …Barry has been performing at various venues for the past few years, most recently at the Mitch Miller Dinner Theater in Branson, Missouri.

BARRY. Wow. You've really done your homework.

LANCE. I was the President of The Synchronistics Fan Club, Maple Valley Branch.

BARRY. That's great.

LANCE. And I'm the proud owner of the only bootleg video tape copy of your first performance you did right here at WKLN twenty years ago. Here it is.

(He holds up the VCR video tape.)

MINDY. That's the only copy?

LANCE. Uh huh. I bought it at an auction in 1981. The next year, the master was destroyed in the great Maple Valley mud slide. Would you guys sign it for me?

EVERYONE. Sure, okay, absolutely, yeah, etc.

LANCE. Awesome!

(He sets the tape on the small table, next to the water bottles, behind him.)

BARRY. Umm, Lance, I just wanna say, it's really nice to be back together again as a group.

*(**MINDY** chuckles. **BARRY** looks at her.)*

Excuse me?

MINDY. Nothing.

(into her mic)

Hi, I'm Mindy. I've been touring while working on a solo album.

*(**BARRY** chuckles. To **BARRY**.)*

I'm sorry?

BARRY. Nothing.

LANCE. *(to the camera)* For those who don't know, Barry and Mindy used to be married...

*(He looks at **BARRY** and **MINDY** who look straight ahead, stone faced.)*

To each other.

CARL. *(changing the subject)* Hey, I see Todd up in the booth, there. Thanks for coming back, there, dude.

(The stage lights blink on and off a couple times.)

Did the lights just blink, or was that me?

LANCE. Todd used to be their roadie, and now he works here. How fun.

BARRY. Thanks for runnin' the sound cues, there, Todd. Just like old times.

LANCE. So, how does it feel to be back together again? Are you as excited as I am?

(CARL is the only one who means it. The others are awkward and insincere.)

EVERYONE. Yeah. Really excited. Big time. Wow. Feels good, incredible, awesome, etc.

MINDY. Umm, Lance, if you don't mind, I'd like to sing one of my favorite songs.

LANCE. Is it "Better Together?"

(He crosses his fingers.)

MINDY. No, it's not. Trust me. This is something I wrote in my motel room in Green Bay, and it was the last song we did as a group before we broke up.

CARL. Just before she destroyed the stage.

LANCE. October 8th, 1979. I was at that concert. After the song, Mindy picked up a speaker and threw it at Barry.

BARRY. She missed.

LANCE. Yeah, but the speaker knocked over a light pole, taking out the drummer.

MINDY. The drummer was unharmed.

PEGGY. Mostly.

LANCE. But the whole stage collapsed. They had to cancel the concert. It was awesome!

(He quickly turns sad.)

Yet, very sad.

CARL. *(emotional)* That was the last time we saw each other.

LANCE. They were supposed to be on Johnny Carson the next night.

CARL. *(gets emotional)* It would have been our big break. Oh, it still hurts.

(holding back tears)

LANCE. *(emotional)* That was the day the music died.

BARRY. *(realizing what song she's talking about)* Yeah, I'm not sure that song is such a good idea.

MINDY. Oh, I think it is.

(She nods to Todd. The music starts.)

LANCE. *(over the music intro, looking around)* We have insurance, don't we?

(He laughs nervously.)

I'm just kidding…Do we?

MINDY. *(sings)*

WE TOURED AROUND THE MIDWEST,
FROM SHEBOYGAN TO CLOQUET,
WE TOURED AROUND THE GREAT LAKES,
TIL IT ENDED IN GREEN BAY.

WE PLAYED THE CLUBS IN OSHKOSH,
EVEN PLAYED OUR WEDDING DAY.
BUT MY WORLD CAME CRASHING DOWN ON ME,
WHEN YOU PLAYED ME IN GREEN BAY.
A HOWARD JOHNSON'S IN GREEN BAY.

OH, WE PLAYED AROUND, YES, WE PLAYED AROUND
TIL I FELL IN LOVE.

BARRY & PEGGY & CARL.

FELL IN LOVE.

MINDY.

WE PLAYED AROUND, OH, WE PLAYED AROUND,
TIL I FELL IN LOVE. UNTIL I FELL IN LOVE WITH YOU.

OUR LIVES WERE PICTURE PERFECT.
WE WERE HAPPY AS CAN BE.
THEN YOU BROKE MY HEART AND
YOU WRECKED MY LIFE WHEN YOU PLAYED AROUND ON ME.

*(**CARL** looks at **PEGGY** who is embarrassed.)*

YOU'RE SUCH A WHOPPING LOSER.
A LOSER ALL THE WAY.
YOU GOT MY BEST FRIEND DRUNK
AND THEN YOU SHTUPPED HER IN GREEN BAY.

*(looks at **PEGGY**)*

A HOWARD JOHNSON'S IN GREEN BAY.
OH, YOU PLAYED AROUND, YEAH, JUST LIKE A HOUND,
YES, YOU PLAYED AROUND.

BARRY & PEGGY & CARL.

PLAYED AROUND.

MINDY.
  YOU PUSHED ME DOWN, TIL I HIT THE GROUND,
  BUT I WILL REBOUND. CAUSE I AM DONE WITH LOVIN' YOU.
EVERYONE.
  DONE WITH YOU.
  DONE WITH YOU.
  DONE WITH YOU.
LANCE. Fantastic! Wow! And to think it's been 20 years since they did that song.

PEGGY. We never got to finish it the first time.

LANCE. Okay, if you like what you're watching, give us a call with your generous pledge.

  (He looks offstage. No callers. He looks back to the camera.)

  No donation is too small.

  (He looks offstage again, then back to the camera.)

  Anything at all. Anything.

  (He looks offstage, then back to the camera.)

  And If you give one hundred dollars or more, you will receive,

  (reads from the card)

  the double album 8-track tape from their "Hands Across the Intersection" tour.

  *(He looks over to **BARRY**.)*

  Eight track tapes? Really? You don't have CD's?

BARRY. We still have a truck load of 8-tracks from the last concert.

LANCE. Super. Hey, why don't you tell us something the fans don't know. Peggy?

PEGGY. *(Taken off guard, she leans into the mic, shy.)* Okay, umm…

  (thinks)

  I sold one of my kidneys for five thousand dollars.

LANCE. Wow!

CARL. They're up to five thousand dollars?

PEGGY. Yeah.

LANCE. The Synchronistics together again! Awesome! Okay, just a reminder, every Friday is Calypso Night at the VFW. Let's go check out the community calendar.

(The "On Air" light goes off.)

STATION MANAGER. *(V.O.)* And we're out.

(Everyone relaxes, going back to their normal "off air" selves.)

LANCE. Guys, I just wanna say that this is a dream come true for me.

MINDY. Oh, you're so sweet. Say, Lance, do you know what time the induction ceremony is gonna be tomorrow?

LANCE. Ceremony?

MINDY. You know, for the Disco Hall of Fame.

BARRY. Our manager said there was a big ground breaking ceremony. He said we're gonna be inducted.

CARL. There's a Disco Hall of Fame?

LANCE. Peggy didn't tell you?

PEGGY. *(trying to act innocent)* Tell 'em what? I don't know anything.

LANCE. Well, actually, the ground breaking won't be until this spring. But the induction will still happen. That's a done deal.

CARL. Alright!

LANCE. Provided the vote goes through tomorrow.

MINDY. What vote?

LANCE. The City Council is voting tomorrow whether to go ahead with the Disco Hall of Fame.

MINDY. Wait, they haven't even decided on it, yet? I thought that's why we were here.

LANCE. Oh, no, don't worry, it's just a formality. They just wanted to see how this telethon went first.

BARRY. So their decision is based on how well we do in this telethon?

LANCE. It's no big deal. Really. We just have to raise the ten thousand dollars, that's all.

MINDY. And what if we don't?

LANCE. Well, then they'll have to close the station. But that won't happen cause, hellooo, you guys rock!!

(gives two "hang loose" hand gestures)

MINDY. They'll close the station if we don't raise the ten thousand dollars?!

LANCE. On a positive note, you can save the station, which means they'll probably vote "yes" on the Disco Hall of Fame tomorrow, which will be a huge boost for the local economy and we really need the money, cause, I mean, this town is going bankrupt. And you're our last hope. So think of it this way, you're gonna be heroes!

(puts his hand up to his ear piece)

Oh, they want me for something. I'll be right back.

(He exits.)

MINDY. *(gritting her teeth)* They lied to us.

CARL. *(to MINDY)* Please don't destroy the studio.

MINDY. *(gritting her teeth)* Don't worry, Carl. I've been taking anger management classes.

PEGGY. I'm feeling a little light headed. I shouldn't have given blood this morning. But twenty bucks *is* twenty bucks.

CARL. Twenty bucks? Sweet! This is awesome!

BARRY. What's awesome?

CARL. Don't you see? If we can pull this off, we'll be heroes, and we might have a chance to tour again. For money.

MINDY. Tour?…He cheated on me!

*(pointing to **PEGGY**)*

With her!!

(Everyone cringes, afraid. **MINDY** *catches herself getting angry. Takes a deep breath, closes her eyes, her hands are in a meditating position. In a soothing voice.)*

MINDY. *(cont.)* I'm a good person, and I deserve to be happy and calm at all times.

(She calms down.)

BARRY. I said I was sorry.

MINDY. Oh, well, okay then. It's all better, now.

BARRY. Really?

MINDY. No! I counted on you, and you broke my heart.

PEGGY. I'm sorry, Mindy. He said you were getting a divorce.

MINDY. Well he got *that* right.

CARL. We're gonna be heroes!

MINDY. I can't believe they lied to us. They told us we were gonna be inducted into the Disco Hall of Fame and they haven't even voted on whether to build it.

CARL. Okay, you know what, now is the time to pull together as a group, because we need each other, alright? And WKLN needs *us*. I mean, they gave us our first break, here, okay, and we owe it to 'em. We could have been big. *Johnny Carson* big. We were right there. And we can get there again, okay, if Mindy agrees to tour.

*(**LANCE** enters.)*

STATION MANAGER. *(V.O.)* And we're live in three, two, one.

(The "On Air" light turns on. They all quickly put on their fake smiles.)

LANCE. *(waving a note card)* We finally got a pledge.

CARL.	**PEGGY.**
Sweet!	Yes!

LANCE. It's from Helen Stromberg. Helen would like to donate

(reading the card)

"twelve donuts."

PEGGY. *(starving for a donut)* Donuts.

LANCE. Thank you, Helen. That's very nice of you. Just a reminder to our viewers, we're looking for *money*.

(**CARL** *raises his hand.*)

Yes, Carl.

CARL. *(into the mic)* Umm...I'd like to acknowledge someone who's, like, watching right now. My mom.

(to the camera)

Hi, Mom. Thanks for lettin' me move back home.

PEGGY. Hi, Mrs. Cosgrove.

CARL. This is a special day cause it's the first time Mom has ever seen me perform. I mean, with Bingo Club and Tupperware she didn't have that many opportunities to see me...

(forcing a smile, getting a little emotional)

Three hundred and ninety-two opportunities, but who's counting? She's watching now, allegedly, and that's what's important.

(to his mom)

I love you, Mom.

(He cries. **PEGGY** *consoles him.)*

BARRY. *(into microphone)* Lance, if it's okay, I'd like to do a song I wrote while we were on hiatus.

LANCE. You're playing it here for the first time?

BARRY. Yeah.

LANCE. Sweet!

BARRY. *(into mic)* You know, forgiveness is possibly the greatest virtue that anyone could ever have.

MINDY. I thought it was fidelity.

LANCE. *(a la Ed McMahon)* Hey-oe!

CARL. *(whispers to* **BARRY** *and* **MINDY**) Keep it together.

BARRY. *(to* **MINDY**) This is from me, to you.

MINDY. Oh, brother.

BARRY. *(looking up to the booth)* Number three, Todd, my disc.

(The music starts.)

BARRY. *(sings)*

MY JUDGEMENT WAS OFF, I MADE A MISTAKE.
DIGGA DUM, DIGGA DUM, DIGGA DUM, DIGGA DUM,
DIGGA DUM, DIGGA DUM, DIGGA DUM.
I BLAME THE LABATTS, I SHOULDN'T PARTAKE.

(BARRY *looks at the others, giving them the cue to come in.)*

EVERYONE.

DIGGA DUM, DIGGA DUM, DIGGA DUM,
DIGGA DUM, DIGGA DUM, DIGGA DUM.

BARRY.

BUT LOOK AT IT FROM MY SIDE.
I WAS TRYIN' TO BE A NICE GUY,
AND GIVE A LONELY GIRL
A CHANCE, TO BE WITH ME.

(PEGGY *reacts.)*

AND I WANT YOU, BUT I HURT YOU,
AND I WANT YOU, BUT I HURT YOU, I KNOW.

EVERYONE.

DIGGA DUM, DIGGA DUM, DIGGA DUM, DIGGA DUM,
DIGGA DUM, DIGGA DUM, DIGGA DUM.

BARRY.

AND I WANT YOU, BUT I HURT YOU,
AND I WANT YOU, DON'T WANT YOU TO GO.

EVERYONE.

DIGGA DUM, DIGGA DUM, DIGGA DUM, DIGGA DUM,
DIGGA DUM, DIGGA DUM.

BARRY.

SO PLEASE FORGIVE ME,
I'LL NEVER BOINK YOUR FRIEND AGAIN.

(PEGGY *reacts.)*

YES, PLEASE FORGIVE ME
I WANNA MAKE AMENDS AND THEN,
I WANNA SLEEP WITH YOU.

CARL & PEGGY.

SLEEP WITH YOU.

BARRY & PEGGY & CARL.

SLEEP WITH YOU...AGAIN.

LANCE. Oh, my gosh! That was so amazing!

(to the camera)

Will Barry and Mindy get back together right here on WKLN?

(He looks at **BARRY** *and* **MINDY** *who are stone faced, then back to the camera.)*

Stay tuned!

(reading a note card)

Now, if you pledge two hundred and fifty dollars or more, you will receive the DVD box set, "The Lawrence Welk Years; The Best of Bobby and Sissy."

(looks over to Erma)

Any calls, Erma?

(We hear Erma's bicycle horn.)

Is that a "no"?

(annoyed, to the booth)

Is she gonna do that?

(puts his hand to his ear piece)

Go to commercial?....There's no commercial?...Public Service Announcement?...There is?

(to the camera)

Okay, we'll be back after these words from the...

(puts his hand to his ear piece)

Maple Valley Syrup Museum. Be sure to take the five minute tour.

(The "On Air" light goes off.)

STATION MANAGER. *(V.O.)* And we're out.

(Everyone relaxes.)

LANCE. *(to the group)* This is so exciting! My contract with Channel 9 is up for renewal this month, and if this goes well, this is the kinda story that will elevate my career to anchorman!

(He exits.)

BARRY. Great. Now we're responsible for Lance's career.

MINDY. *(to BARRY)* So…you're sorry that you "boinked" my friend?

BARRY. Yes, I am.

MINDY. And now you wanna sleep with me again?

BARRY. Yes, I do.

MINDY. Uh huh…

(sarcastic)

I am so sorry I over-reacted.

BARRY. Hey, I was partially to blame.

(She rolls her eyes and walks offstage.)

Where are you going?

MINDY. I need a cigarette.

BARRY. *(following her out)* I thought you quit.

MINDY. I just started again.

(MINDY and BARRY are gone, leaving PEGGY and CARL on stage alone.)

CARL. *(to PEGGY)* I forgive you.

PEGGY. *(taken off guard)* I'm sorry. What?

CARL. For breaking up our group, and sending me on a spiritual journey.

PEGGY. Carl, I am really sorry about that, okay. It was a low point in my life, and…"spiritual journey?"

CARL. Thanks for asking. After Green Bay, things got kinda tough for me. I hit the bottle pretty hard, and other recreational things, and then one day, after waking up in a dumpster behind a 7-Eleven, I knew I needed to get my life back together.

PEGGY. Well, good for you.

(She goes over to the table with the water bottles.)

CARL. So I shaved my head, became a Moonie, and moved to India where I lived in a mud hut with a chicken named Javier. I learned more in India than anything I ever learned in 5th grade. Both times. I'm talking about love, about caring, but mostly I'm talking about bathing with seaweed in the Gulf of Horackkkkkkkkkk.

(Sounds like he's got a hair caught in his throat.)

PEGGY. *(to herself)* I wonder how much I could get for my appendix.

CARL. *(from out of nowhere)* I love you.

PEGGY. *(casual, like "just friends" love)* Oh, that's sweet, Carl. I love you, too.

CARL. No, no, it's not like that. It's not like brother-sister love, it's...it's man love...Manly man love. The kind of man love that makes me wanna be with you...in a manly way.

PEGGY. *(thinks)* I thought you were gay.

CARL. *(groans)* Ahh!...One indiscreet night on Fire Island and you're labeled for life.

PEGGY. It was more like a month.

CARL. I was confused! But I'm not now.

(looks at the camera)

Mom, I'm not confused anymore. Really. I read L. Ron Hubbard.

PEGGY. *(picking up the video tape)* I bet this video tape is worth something.

(She looks around to see if anyone is watching, contemplating taking it.)

CARL. *(looks at the camera)* I love her, Mom. She's a great girl, isn't she? Look at her. She looks like you when you were young...There may be some issues with that, I know.

PEGGY. Carl, I don't think we're on the air.

(She sets the tape down.)

CARL. I've been thinking about you for, like, twenty years.

PEGGY. Really? Carl, that's very sweet, but we don't really know each other. I mean, we were in Home Ec. together, and made carrot cake and everything, and then we toured, but we never really hung out or anything, and,

(quickly changing thoughts)

you're not gay?

CARL. No, I'm just a snappy dresser…Look, you'll get to know me, okay? I mean, I know *you.*

*(***PEGGY*** looks at* **CARL,** *nervous.)*

STATION MANAGER. *(V.O.)* And we're live in three, two, one.

(The "On Air" light goes on. **LANCE** *enters.* **PEGGY** *and* **CARL** *quickly smile.)*

LANCE. Welcome back to the WKLN…

(looking at **CARL** *and* **PEGGY***)*

Where's Barry and Mindy?

CARL. Lance, if it's okay, I'd like to sing a love song I wrote after eating curry with the Dalai Lama.

LANCE. You know the Dalai Lama?

CARL. Yeah, we partied.

*(***CARL*** looks up to Todd in the booth, holds up five fingers and mouths, "five." The music starts.)*

CARL. *(sings)*

    I LOVE THE WAY YOU WALK,
    AND I LOVE THE WAY YOU TALK.
    AND I LOVE YOU ALL THE TIME.
    WISH YOU WERE MINE.

    I LOVE YOU AFTER SCHOOL,
    WATCH YOU GO FROM HOT TO COOL.
    AS I PEEK BETWEEN THE FENCE POST,
    JUST TO WATCH YOU FROLIC IN YOUR SWIMMING POOL.

    (As the song progresses, **PEGGY** *gets more and more uneasy.)*

I WATCH YOU AS YOU EAT.
WITH YOUR FAMILY, EATING MEAT.
AND I WATCH YOU DO YOUR HOMEWORK,
THRU YOUR BEDROOM WINDOW PAIN.

I WATCH YOU AS YOU SMILE.
WITH YOUR STUFFED TOY CROCODILE,
THAT YOU HOLD LIKE A BABY SHEEP,
 WHILE YOU ARE FAST ASLEEP.

AND THAT'S WHY I FOLLOWED YOU HOME.

*(He looks at **PEGGY**, prodding her to repeat the line. She takes his cue.)*

PEGGY.

THAT'S WHY HE FOLLOWED ME HOME.

CARL.

TO LOVE YOU FROM AFAR.

PEGGY.

TO LOVE ME FROM AFAR.

CARL.

AND BE WITH YOU EVERY DAY.
I TOOK SOME PICTURES, HERE THEY ARE.

(He takes photos from his pocket and holds them out to her.)

THAT'S WHY I FOLLOWED YOU HOME.

PEGGY.

THAT'S WHY HE FOLLOWED ME HOME.

CARL.

SO I COULD WATCH YOU.

PEGGY.

WATCH ME.

CARL.

WATCH YOU.
CAUSE I LOVE YOU. THAT MUCH.

I love you, Peggy, more than all the hashish in Turkey.

*(**LANCE** reaches offstage and grabs a card.)*

LANCE. Fantastic! Wow! We just got our first real pledge.

PEGGY. Awesome!

LANCE. *(reading the card)* One hundred dollars from the American Voyeur Society.

(He moves the thermometer up to $100.)

CARL. Voyeurs rock! Yeah, I don't know what that is.

LANCE. And at this pace, we'll reach our goal in three months.

(He laughs.)

I'm just kidding. We'll get there...

*(Looks at **CARL** and **PEGGY** with a nervous, uncertain look.)*

Right?

(Erma's bicycle horn honks. To the camera, re: the annoying horn.)

Excuse me.

*(**LANCE** steps offstage. We hear a horn honk. He steps back on stage holding Erma's horn from her walker.)*

*(**CARL** gets down on one knee, as if to propose to **PEGGY**. **MINDY** enters, followed by **BARRY**.)*

BARRY. *(to **MINDY**)* Mindy, think of the money we can make...

MINDY. *(seeing **CARL** on his knee)* ...Shh.

LANCE. *(re: **CARL** on his knee)* What's this?

PEGGY. *(to **CARL**)* Oh, no, wait, okay, no, now, just, okay what are you doing?

*(**CARL** takes out a ring box from his pocket. He opens it and holds it out to **PEGGY**.)*

CARL. Peggy, will you marry me?

LANCE. *(to the camera)* Are we getting this?! Are we getting this?!

PEGGY. Oh gosh, oh gosh, oh gosh.

(looks in the box)

There's no ring in that box.

CARL. It's on layaway.

MINDY. Make sure you get a better divorce lawyer than I did, honey.

CARL. Sorry, Mom. I was gonna tell you earlier, but you were watching "SmackDown."

PEGGY. You don't wanna marry me, Carl. I've got baggage.

CARL. Is it Samsonite? Cause that's quality stuff.

LANCE. Looks like we're getting a call. Stay tuned for Peggy's answer! Let's go to the phone.

(The "On Air" light goes off.)

STATION MANAGER. *(V.O.)* And we're out.

(Everyone relaxes.)

LANCE. A Synchronistics marriage proposal live on WKLN! This is the greatest day of my life!

(He exits with the bicycle horn, leaving it offstage.)

BARRY. I think a wedding would be great! It'll kick off our reunion tour.

MINDY. There isn't gonna *be* a reunion tour.

PEGGY. *(to herself)* I'm too old to sell my eggs anymore… Oh, that was good money.

MINDY. Besides, you don't even need to tour.

CARL. I do.

PEGGY. So do I.

MINDY. *(to* **BARRY***)* All the money you're making on the publishing rights to "Better Together."

BARRY. You know, maybe we should do "Better Together." I mean, it is our one hit, and it might help us get donations.

MINDY. We are not doing "Better Together!!"

(Catching herself getting angry. Takes a deep breath, closes her eyes, her hands are in a meditating position. In a soothing voice.)

I deserve to be happy and calm at all times.

(She calms down.)

*(***LANCE*** enters with a note card.)*

STATION MANAGER. *(V.O.)* And we're live in three, two, one.

(The "On Air" light goes on. Everyone quickly puts on their fake smiles.)

LANCE. We're back, and we have a question from a caller. Not a pledge, but a question. Amanda would like to know,

(reading the card)

"How did you get started as a group?"

(looking offstage)

I know this one. Can I answer? No? Let them? Okay.

BARRY. Well, we actually met in choir right here at Maple Valley High School.

CARL. Go Fighting Syrup!…

EVERYONE. *(They all "press" the waffle.)* Waffle 'em!

CARL. *(stating the obvious)* We were the Fighting Syrup.

BARRY. Carl was a little older.

CARL. Eighth grade was the best five years of my life.

BARRY. We all thought he was the janitor.

CARL. Actually, I was.

BARRY. I didn't know Mindy at the time, but when I saw her whistle the theme song from Rocky while doing an interpretive dance of Mark Spitz winning seven gold medals in the '72 Olympics…I knew I found my soul mate.

MINDY. *(whispers to* **CARL** *and* **PEGGY***)* Anyone have a shovel?

LANCE. Barry, is it true that you "discovered" Mindy?

MINDY. *(whispers to* **CARL** *and* **PEGGY***)* Here we go.

BARRY. I don't know if I would say "discovered." It was more like helping Mindy realize how talented she was. I mean, I just really believed in her and I think that helped her gain confidence, and once that happened, she really discovered *herself.*

*(***MINDY*** rolls her eyes.)*

LANCE. I heard you got Mindy into her first play.

BARRY. Yeah, it wasn't easy. Mindy was pretty shy back then, she didn't wanna do it, but I finally convinced her to play Juliet to my Romeo in the school play. It was the only way I could get her to kiss me.

PEGGY. Oh, that's so sweet.

MINDY. Oh, high school back then was such a great time, wasn't it? When love was innocent and true. And then the deceit train pulled into betrayal town.

(She looks at **BARRY.**)

BARRY. *(ignoring her dig)* After Romeo and Juliet, Mindy got the lead in every school play. Oh, she was mesmerizing. So what happened, all the guys were hitting on her, right, and I didn't wanna lose her so I suggested we start an a cappella group with Carl and Peggy.

MINDY. We called ourselves "The Four Windpipes."

EVERYONE. *(singing)*
WINDPIPES.

BARRY. But "The Four Windpipes" didn't really capture how well we worked together.

*(***MINDY** *chuckles.)*

So we changed our name to "The Synchronistics."

CARL. Whoa. When did we change our name?

LANCE. Looks like Carl had a little too much hippie lettuce, huh?

(He laughs, then is serious. To **CARL.**)

You got any on you?

(He laughs.)

I'm just kidding.

(Serious. Whispers to **CARL.**)

Do you?…Cause there's just so much pressure.

(looking offstage, touching his ear piece)

What?…The proposal? Right, we haven't heard Peggy's answer.

CARL. *(taking her hand while kneeling)* Peggy, will you...

    (forgot what he was going to ask)

    What was I gonna ask?

PEGGY. Carl, I'm not the right person for you.

CARL. You are, too. I have pictures.

    (He holds out the photos to her.)

MINDY. Lance, I'd like to do a song about relationships.

LANCE. Is it "Better Togeth...

MINDY. *(cutting him off)* ...No.

LANCE. Okay.

MINDY. This is a true story.

    (looks up to the booth and nods to Todd)

    The music starts.

MINDY. *(ad lib, spoken.)*

    IN THE BATTLE OF THE SEXES
    FROM THE TIME OF LYSISTRATA
    WHEN WOMEN HAD ENOUGH OF MEN
    TO SEX THEY JUST SAID "NADA."

PEGGY. That means, "no."

MINDY. *(singing)*

    THE WAY I FEEL RIGHT NOW,
    MEN LEAVE ME COLD AS ICICLES,

PEGGY. But you look hot.

MINDY.

    I BELIEVE THAT WOMEN DO NEED MEN,
    'BOUT AS MUCH AS FISH NEED BICYCLES.

BARRY. *(whispers to* **MINDY***)* This is not my favorite song.

MINDY. *(whispers back)* You brought it upon yourself.

    I WANT

MINDY & PEGGY.

    NO MORE MEN,

MINDY.

    I DON'T BELIEVE IN BARBIE 'N KEN,
    I WANT

MINDY & PEGGY.

NO MORE MEN.

MINDY.

I'D BE MUCH HAPPIER THEN

WITHOUT ANY MORE MEN.

BARRY. *(whispers to* **MINDY***)* So, what? You never dated after we broke up?

MINDY. *(whispers back)* What do you care?

I WANT

MINDY & PEGGY.

NO MORE MEN,

MINDY.

I'LL SAY IT OVER AGAIN.

I WANT

MINDY & PEGGY.

NO MORE MEN.

MINDY.

I'D RATHER BE A DODDERIN' HEN,

THAN HAVE ANY MORE MEN.

BARRY. *(whispers to* **MINDY***)* For your information, I care a lot, okay?

MINDY. *(whispers back)* You care a lot about touring.

I NEED A LITTLE TIME FOR ME.

TO JUST PLAY OR GO CLIMB A TREE.

I'D FEEL LOWER THAN OLD POND SCUM,

THAN TO LIVE MY LIFE UNDER THE THUMB OF MEN.

BARRY. *(whispers to* **MINDY***)* You were never under my thumb.

MINDY. *(whispers back)* Your thumb has my face print on it!

(She calms down.)

I WANT

MINDY & PEGGY.

NO MORE MEN,

MINDY.

I'LL SAY IT OVER AGAIN,

I WANT

MINDY & PEGGY.

    NO MORE MEN.

MINDY.

    I'D RATHER BE A LESBIAN

    THAN HAVE ANY MORE...

MINDY & PEGGY.

    NO MORE MEN,

MINDY.

    I'LL WRITE IT DOWN WITH A FOUNTAIN PEN.

    I WANT

MINDY & PEGGY.

    NO MORE MEN,

MINDY.

    I'D RATHER DATE A MARY OR JEN

    THAN A LARRY OR BEN.

MINDY & PEGGY.

    NO MORE MEN.

    *(**LANCE** reaches offstage and grabs a card.)*

LANCE. Awesome! Alright! We just got four hundred dollars from the Maple Valley Lady Bikers Club!

    (He moves the thermometer up to $500.)

CARL. Biker chicks!

PEGGY. Go Schwinn!

LANCE. They like your argument songs.

    *(whispers to **BARRY**)*

    Do more of those.

    (to the camera)

    Let's go visit Erma.

    (The "On Air" light goes off.)

STATION MANAGER. *(V.O.)* And we're out.

    (Everyone relaxes.)

LANCE. You guys are the best!

MINDY. Um, Lance, I was wondering how we could have been mistaken about the induction ceremony tomorrow.

LANCE. Peggy, do you wanna tell 'em?

PEGGY. Tell 'em what? I don't know anything.

BARRY. It'll be fine, Mindy. Really. It'll all work out.

LANCE. *(puts his hand to his ear piece, looking offstage)* We're getting a call? Okay.

(to the group)

I'll be right back.

(He exits.)

BARRY. *(to MINDY)* So you've completely given up on men. Is that it?

MINDY. Not entirely. I mean, I have trust issues that have kept me from falling in love. Thank you for that, by the way, and, oh yeah, speaking of which…why did you cheat on me?

BARRY. My therapist said it was because I didn't think I was good enough for you, and I was afraid you'd leave me for someone better, so I sabotaged our relationship.

CARL. Whoa. A pre-emptive strike.

MINDY. You thought I'd leave you?

BARRY. Yeah.

MINDY. Did I ever give you a reason to think that?

(BARRY doesn't have an answer.)

CARL. *(to PEGGY)* Okay, they're workin' it out, I can tell. And we can too, Peggy. I know it's a big step but I really wanna share the rest of my life with you, for better or worse, rain or shine, or a cavity search in Bangkok.

PEGGY. *(ponders that for a beat)* I have a child.

(Everyone looks at PEGGY.)

CARL. Already? We haven't even kissed, yet.

MINDY. How old is your child?

PEGGY. He's nineteen.

CARL. *(excited)* "He?" It's a boy! We have a boy!

BARRY. He's nineteen?

PEGGY. Yeah.

CARL. *(Excited. Oblivious.)* This is awesome! I can get him a Happy Meal!

BARRY. *(putting it together)* Wait, so…did you go out with someone after we…you know.

PEGGY. No.

BARRY. Uh huh. Did you, ahh…did you do that test tube baby deal?

PEGGY. No.

MINDY. He's yours, ya dunce!

CARL. Oh, man, this is totally trippy.

BARRY. *(to PEGGY)* Why didn't you tell me?

PEGGY. You don't wanna be a father.

BARRY. How do you know?

(**PEGGY** *doesn't respond.*)

CARL. What's his name?

PEGGY. His name is "Manilow,"

(sings the Barry Manilow song, "Mandy.")

"OH, MANDY, WELL YOU CAME AND YOU GAVE…"

MINDY. …Yeah, we got it.

CARL. *(to PEGGY)* I'm so happy for you…

(getting emotional)

And for Barry's Manilow.

BARRY. Are you sure he's mine?

PEGGY. Yeah. He has your ego.

CARL. He needs a man in his life. A father.

MINDY. No, he doesn't. He's a grown up.

CARL. Everyone needs a man in his life. And I'd love to be his man. We can go swimming at the Y, and sing show tunes.

(He looks up, visualizing it. Everyone reacts to CARL. He snaps out of it.)

Unless Barry wants to.

BARRY. Yeah, you know, I've got a lot on my plate right now, and…

PEGGY. Well, there you have it.

BARRY. *(to* **MINDY***)* This isn't gonna hurt our chances of going on tour, is it?

MINDY. *(sarcastic)* Nooooo!

BARRY. Right, right, okay. You know what. I'm gonna go ahead, there, and do the right thing, step up to the plate, and...

(He swallows.)

be the fa...the father to your nineteen year-old child.

PEGGY. *(thinks)* No, thanks.

BARRY. Wait a minute. You don't want my help? You don't need money?

PEGGY. Yes, I do. But I'd rather do it on my own.

BARRY. *(getting upset)* You can't deny me the right to help support my son.

PEGGY. You weren't that interested a minute ago.

BARRY. Yeah, well, that's before you denied me.

MINDY. *(re:* **BARRY***)* This is what I had to deal with.

STATION MANAGER. *(V.O.)* And we're live in three, two, one.

*(***LANCE*** steps back onto stage. The "On Air" light goes on. Everyone quickly puts on a fake smile.)*

LANCE. Welcome back...

PEGGY. ...Lance, I'd like to sing a song I wrote about my little man-child.

LANCE. You have a man-child? I'm gonna win a Pulitzer for this!

*(***PEGGY*** looks up to the booth and nods to Todd. The music starts.)*

CARL. *(over the music intro, to* **BARRY** *and* **MINDY***)* Peggy wrote a song. Awesome!

PEGGY. *(sings)*
I GAVE BIRTH TO A LITTLE MAN-CHILD,
A TWELVE POUND BABY BOY.
HOW I CRIED WHEN I HAD MY MAN-CHILD,
A TWENTY-THREE INCH LONG BUNDLE OF JOY.

PEGGY. *(cont.)*

> I RAISED HIM BY MYSELF AND I WILL,
> SAY NO THANKS TO YOU.
>
> *(to* **BARRY***)*
>
> HE WAS SAD HE HAD NO DADDY,
> SOMEONE HE COULD LOOK UP TO.
>
> HOW I LOVE MY LITTLE MAN-CHILD.

CARL & MINDY & BARRY.

> MAN CHILD.

PEGGY.

> I CAN'T LOVE HIM ENOUGH.
> HE'S A MAN, MY LITTLE MAN-CHILD.

CARL & MINDY & BARRY.

> MAN CHILD.

PEGGY.

> I HOPE TO SEE HIM SOON ENOUGH.
>
> EVEN THOUGH HE'S NOW IN PRISON,
>
> *(***BARRY*** reacts.)*
>
> I LOVE HIM A-LOT.
> HE'S MY CHILD, MY LITTLE MAN-CHILD
> DOIN' THREE TO FIVE FOR POT.
> Don't do drugs.

CARL. Just say, "maybe."

PEGGY.

> HOW I LOVE MY LITTLE MAN-CHILD.

CARL & MINDY & BARRY.

> MAN CHILD.

PEGGY.

> I LOVE HIS TATTOOED FACE.
> HE'S A MELANCHOLY MAN-CHILD.

CARL & MINDY & BARRY.

> MAN CHILD.

PEGGY.

> HE'LL SOON BE IN A HAPPY PLACE.
> TODAY HE'S BREAKING OUT OF PRISON, TO FIND HIS DAD.

WHEN HE FINDS HIM, HE WILL BEAT HIM.
LIKE A SNARE DRUM, THEN HE'LL BE GLAD.

LANCE. Fantastic! Wow! Peggy's first song on WKLN!

(He looks offstage left.)

What's this?

(He leans offstage and grabs a note card.)

We just got four hundred dollars from the Maple Valley Depression Clinic.

(He moves the thermometer up to $900.)

CARL. Go Prozac!

LANCE. *(looking off toward Erma)* Hey, it looks like we got another caller!...Where's Erma?...On a smoke break?...

(despondent)

Yeah, I'll get it.

(He reaches offstage, grabs a phone, brings it out and holds it to his ear.)

WKLN...

(changing his tone)

I told you never to call me at work.

(The "On Air" light goes off.)

STATION MANAGER. *(V.O.)* And we're out.

(Everyone relaxes. LANCE exits.)

BARRY. Peggy, is your son really breaking out of prison to find me and beat me?

PEGGY. No. I told him you were dead.

BARRY. Thank you.

PEGGY. That was just my dream.

MINDY. But, he *is* in prison, right?

PEGGY. Actually, he got out last week on good behavior.

CARL. Righteous.

PEGGY. He's watching from home in the trailer.

(playing with him)

PEGGY. *(cont.)* So don't make me mad.

BARRY. *(smiling uncomfortably)* I won't.

CARL. We have to celebrate.

MINDY. Celebrate what?

CARL. Peggy's son is out of prison!

EVERYONE. *(insincere)* Yeah, sure, we'll celebrate, whatever, brilliant idea, etc.

CARL. Hey, whoa! I detect insincerity, there. Dudes, we are professionals, alright, and no matter what happens today, we can not lose our funky stuff. Okay?

EVERYONE. *(equally as insincere as before)* Yeah, okay, fine, professionals, funky stuff, we got it, whatever, etc.

(LANCE enters.)

STATION MANAGER. *(V.O.)* And we're live in three, two, one.

(The "On Air" light goes on. Everyone quickly smiles.)

LANCE. We are back…

CARL. …Lance, if it's okay with you, we'd like to get on board the funk train.

(CARL nods to Todd in the booth. The music starts.)

LANCE. Oh, my gosh! I love this song! Can I sing along? Please?

CARL. Sure.

LANCE. Alright!

EVERYONE. *(big fake smiles, singing)*
PUT YOUR HANDS ON YOUR HIPS,
THEN TURN TO THE RIGHT.
THROW SOME COAL ON THE FIRE,
WE'LL BE DANCIN' ALL NIGHT.

ON THE FUNK TRAIN.
OO-AH, OO-AH.
ON THE FUNK TRAIN.
OO-AH, OO-AH.
HEAR THE ENGINE ROAR,
PUT THE THROTTLE TO THE FLOOR,
ON THE FUNK TRAIN.

PEGGY. Do it!

(Dance sequence.)

EVERYONE.

PUT THE COW CATCHER ON.
THEN THROW ON THE COAL.
WE'RE SPEEDIN' DOWN THE TRACK.
WE'RE OUTTA CONTROL.

ON THE FUNK TRAIN.
OO-AH, OO-AH.
ON THE FUNK TRAIN.
OO-AH, OO-AH.

*(***LANCE*** exits.)*

GET YOUR FUNKY ON,
WE ARE DANCIN' DUSK TIL DAWN,
ON THE FUNK TRAIN.

MINDY. Do the Hustle!

*(Dance sequence. ***LANCE*** enters carrying a little disco ball on a string and a flashlight. He dances around with the group while shining the light on the spinning ball.)*

EVERYONE.

WHEN YA FEEL KINDA DOWN,
AND YOU LOST YOUR FUNK,
GET A TICKET TO THE FUNK TRAIN,
AND START SHAKIN' YOUR JUNK.

ON THE FUNK TRAIN.
OO-AH, OO-AH.
ON THE FUNK TRAIN.
 OO-AH, OO-AH.
WON'T YA CLIMB ON BOARD,
ALL YOUR FUNK WILL BE RESTORED,
ON THE FUNK TRAIN.

FUNK TRAIN!

LANCE. *(to the camera)* Look at me. I'm the caboose! OO-AH, OO-AH! Anyone with me?…No? Okay…

(He looks offstage.)

LANCE. *(cont.)* What?…Oh, look, the phone is lighting up.

    (He exits with the disco ball and flashlight.)

    (The "On Air" light goes off.)

STATION MANAGER. *(V.O.)* And we're out.

    (Everyone relaxes.)

BARRY. I can't believe we still remember the choreography.

CARL. It's like riding a bike without a helmet.

PEGGY. You can leave disco, but disco never leaves you…

    (wistfully)

    Dammit.

    (She goes to the table to get water.)

CARL. This is totally awesome! It's like we're back together!

MINDY. *(sarcastic)* Oh, yeah, that's exactly what I wanna do. Get back together with my ex-husband who cheated on me with my best friend and had a prison-man-baby with her.

BARRY. I had one indiscretion. Do I have to pay for it for the rest of my life?

MINDY. Yeah.

CARL. Come on, Mindy, we all make mistakes. But we forgave Milli Vanilli.

EVERYONE. *(They think for a beat.)* Not so much, not really, no we didn't, etc.

CARL. And that's what it's all about; forgiveness, and a warm chai tea with a hint of paprika…

BARRY. …Carl, focus.

CARL. And money. Because we really need the money.

PEGGY. I'm running out of organs.

BARRY. I had a little drinking problem, okay, and I made a mistake. One indiscretion.

MINDY. That was the only time you cheated on me?

BARRY. The only time. That was it. I'm sorry.

PEGGY. I'm broke, Mindy.

BARRY. Say something.

(PEGGY picks up the video tape from the table and tries to put it in her dress.)

MINDY. Did you quit drinking?

BARRY. Yes...

(He sees PEGGY with the tape.)

Careful, Peggy, that's valuable.

(PEGGY is busted.)

MINDY. *(thinks)* Okay, if we raise the ten thousand dollars, we'll go on tour.

CARL. Yes!

PEGGY. Alright!

(PEGGY puts the tape down.)

CARL. Thank you! We're healing!

MINDY. Don't push it, Carl.

CARL. Dudes, dudettes, we had such great times together, alright, and we'll get that back, okay. If we all just say a good memory we had when we were together, we can complete the healing process. I'll go first...

(thinks)

Okay, umm, my favorite memory was way back when Peggy said she had a son.

PEGGY. *(ponders that)* Carl, that was ten minutes ago.

CARL. *(thinks)* Who's next?

(No one says anything.)

Come on, it's like cleansing your moon shakra with a high colonic from the River of Knowledge...Peggy?

PEGGY. Okay...umm...Well, I guess my favorite memory is singing, and...having money, and...an indoor bathroom.

CARL. Will you marry me?

PEGGY. Carl, I...I'm dating someone.

CARL. Really? Who?

PEGGY. Umm…one of my drivers' training students.

CARL. You mean, like a fifteen year-old?

PEGGY. Well, he didn't tell me how old he was.

CARL. *(holding back the tears)* I don't know why I even let myself get close.

PEGGY. I'm sorry.

CARL. *(barely containing his tears)* I'll be fine…

> *(To himself, trying to keep it in. Chanting:)*

> HARI KRISHNA, HARI KRISHNA.

> *(barely composing himself)*

> Okay…so…Mindy, your turn. Tell us a good memory you have when we were together.

MINDY. I can't think of one.

CARL. You can, too. Come on.

> *(BARRY looks at her with puppy dog eyes.)*

MINDY. Okay…umm…It was after our first concert in Grover City and Barry saw some flowers in a park and picked them for me.

PEGGY. Oh, how romantic.

MINDY. Yeah. They were beautiful.

PEGGY. Ohh.

BARRY. *(endearing)* They arrested me for de-facing public property.

PEGGY. *(emotional)* Oh, that is so sweet.

MINDY. *(lovingly)* Yeah.

CARL. *(holding back tears)* Oh, there go the flood gates… okay…alright, Barry. You're up, dude. Tell us a good memory you have.

BARRY. *(thinks)* Okay…umm…Oh, yeah, after our Gainesville concert, I took Mindy to Lake Okeechobee and we went skinny dipping, and then, well…

> *(to MINDY)*

> you know the rest.

MINDY. That wasn't me!

BARRY. Crap!

MINDY. *(trying to calm herself down)* I deserve to be happy and calm...oh, to hell with it.

CARL. And that's why we have to remember the good times we had, and especially who we had them with.

(LANCE enters, depressed.)

STATION MANAGER. *(V.O.)* And we're live in three, two, one.

LANCE. We just lost four hundred dollars from the Maple Valley Depression Clinic.

CARL. *(depressed, quietly)* Zoloft.

LANCE. *(He moves the thermometer down to $500.)* They didn't like your happy Funk Train song. I guess it was bad for business.

MINDY. Can they do that? Can they take money away?

BARRY. Lance, we'd like to do a song we used to sing to cheer us up.

LANCE. Wait, are you sure? 'Cause they just took money away, 'cause...

BARRY. ...Yeah, it'll be fine. Really. This is something that helped us remember the good times, and forget the bad, because the good times were good, and the bad times...they were not good.

(He nods to Todd in the booth.)

(The music starts.)

BARRY. *(sings)*
YOU WERE THE PROM QUEEN OF MY HEART.
AND I NEVER, NEVER, NEVER, NEVER WANTED TO PART.
SO DON'T YOU TAKE YOUR LOVE AWAY,
BUT HOLD ME CLOSE AND TREAT ME TO YOUR LIP BUFFET.

EVERYONE.
AND REMEMBER THE GOOD TIMES WE HAD.
THE GOOD TIMES WERE BETTER, WERE BETTER THAN BAD.
THE BAD TIMES WILL JUST MAKE YOU SAD.
SO JUST REMEMBER THE GOOD TIMES, AND BE GLAD.

BARRY. *(cont.)*

> YOU WERE THE STARSKY TO MY HUTCH.
> AND IF YOU LEAVE ME I WILL CRY BECAUSE I LOVE YOU SO MUCH.
> YOU WERE THE MINDY TO MY MORK.
> AND WHEN WE KISS YOUR LIPS ARE TASTY AS A PIECE OF ROAST PORK.

PEGGY. Oh, yum.

EVERYONE.

> SO REMEMBER THE GOOD TIMES WE HAD.
> THE GOOD TIMES WERE BETTER, WERE BETTER THAN BAD.
> THE BAD TIMES WILL JUST MAKE YOU SAD.
> SO JUST REMEMBER THE GOOD TIMES,
> JUST REMEMBER THE GOOD TIMES,
> JUST REMEMBER THE GOOD TIMES,

MINDY. I slept with Carl!

BARRY. You what?!

MINDY. I slept with Carl.

CARL. You did?

MINDY. He was great, by the way.

CARL. I was?

MINDY. I couldn't keep it a secret any longer.

CARL. You couldn't?

BARRY. *(to CARL, in slow motion)* I will kill you!

> *(He grabs CARL by the throat and takes him to the floor, choking him.)*

LANCE. *(in slow motion)* Noooo!

> *(Everyone moves in slow motion until the last line of the song which PEGGY and MINDY sing in regular time.)*

PEGGY & MINDY.

> AND BE GLAD.
>
> *(blackout)*

End of Act I

ACT II

(Everyone is offstage.)

*(**LANCE** enters the stage with a glass of Scotch and takes a sip.)*

LANCE. *(looking offstage, holding his hand up to his ear piece)* They're coming back, aren't they? Please tell me they're coming back.

(He takes another sip of Scotch and sets it offstage, hiding it. Defensively.)

It's ice tea! I'm drinking ice tea!

(to himself)

There's just so much pressure.

STATION MANAGER. *(V.O.)* And we're live in three...

LANCE. *(looking offstage)* What's that?

(He leans offstage, grabs a note card then comes back on stage.)

STATION MANAGER. *(V.O.)* Two...one.

(The "On Air" light turns on.)

LANCE. We're back, and...

(reading from the note card)

Oh, my gosh! We just got one thousand dollars from the Maple Valley Association of Divorce Attorneys.

PEGGY. *(offstage)* Awesome!

LANCE. It says here, "The Synchronistics could be our poster child." Alright, they like it when they argue. Just another eight thousand dollars to hit the goal, and less than an hour to do it. Do you believe in miracles?

(LANCE looks doubtful. The music starts. LANCE sneaks a sip of Scotch, then moves the thermometer up to $1,500.)

(The four enter and move to their mics, wearing different outfits than the first act. CARL is wearing a neck brace. There's tension between them.)

EVERYONE. *(singing)*
WE WILL DANCE TIL WE DROP
AND WE'RE NEVER GONNA STOP
UNTIL WE REACH OUR GOAL,

BARRY, PEGGY & CARL.
REACH OUR GOAL.

EVERYONE.
GONNA FIND US A GROOVE
GONNA BUST OUT A MOVE
WE'RE GONNA TAKE CONTROL.
WE'RE THE DANCE PATROL.

A FUNKTASTIC DANCE
THE PERFECT CHANCE
TO MAKE A COSMIC SPLASH.
IT'S A DANCIN' SPREE
IN SYNCHRONICITY
TO RAISE A LOT OF CASH.

SYNCHRONISTIC DANCIN'

BARRY & CARL.
WE'LL SHOW YA HOW

EVERYONE.
SYNCHRONISTIC DANCIN'

BARRY & CARL.
GET READY NOW

MINDY & PEGGY.
WE'LL GO BALLISTIC DANCIN'

EVERYONE.
WE'LL DANCE OUR PANTS AWAY, AWAY, AWAY, AWAY!

*(**NOTE:** During the dance sequence, **LANCE** yells out a dance and the actors do it. As an alternative to the*

following dances, during intermission, you can take suggestions from the audience for fictitious dances, then have **LANCE** *call those out for the actors to perform as an improvisational dance.)*

LANCE. Do the Pogo. The Buckin' Bronco. Feed the Chicken. Burp the Baby.

EVERYONE.
PUT OUR HELMETS ON
WE'RE GONNA DANCE TIL DAWN
OR AT LEAST UNTIL WE LOSE
THERE IS NO EXCUSE
WE MUST LET LOOSE
THE POWER OF OUR SHOES.
SYNCHRONISTIC DANCIN'

BARRY & CARL.
WE'LL SHOW YA HOW

EVERYONE.
WE'RE THE SYNCHRONISTICS DANCIN'

BARRY & CARL.
GET READY NOW

EVERYONE.
RAISIN' CASH WITH OUR MYSTIC DANCIN'
WE'LL DANCE OUR PANTS AWAY AWAY AWAY AWAY!

LANCE. *(to the camera)* Fantastic! Wow! The Synchronistics are back! Let's go to the phone!

(The "On Air" light goes off.)

STATION MANAGER. *(V.O.)* And we're out.

(Everyone relaxes.)

LANCE. You can do it, guys I know you can. No pressure, I just really need this, that's all. Okay.

(He exits.)

BARRY. I just wanna apologize to Carl for my behavior. And I wanna say, in my defense, I don't remember Gainesville very well, okay, that whole skinny dipping deal, and I can't be accountable for anything I did when I was drunk.

MINDY. It's okay. I'm over it. I really am. Let's just finish the telethon, make ten thousand dollars for the station and go our separate ways.

CARL. This is, like, totally harshing my mellow.

BARRY. *(to MINDY)* And now I think *you* should apologize.

MINDY. For what?

BARRY. For sleeping with Carl.

MINDY. What do you mean? *You* slept with Peggy. We're even.

BARRY. "Even?" Oh, no…No, no, no, no, no…We're not even close to being even. We are waaaaay not even. I mean, what you did was sooooo…worse than what I did.

MINDY. Why?

BARRY. Because…

(thinks)

I'm the man.

MINDY. Oh, jeez.

BARRY. And men are expected to do stuff like that.

MINDY. Lovely.

BARRY. And *you're* the woman, so *you* should know better. Shame on you.

MINDY. You're kidding, right?

BARRY. No. It's our society. Our society dictates that men behave that way. It encourages men to sleep with other women. And since women dictate the terms of our society, it's your fault.

(to CARL and PEGGY)

Am I right? Huh? Huh?

CARL. *(uncertain, looking at* **PEGGY***)*	**PEGGY.** *(uncertain, looking at* **CARL***)*
Yes…no…I don't know.	No…yes…maybe…what?

BARRY. *(to MINDY)* So, you see, it's not my fault. Society is to blame. And *you*, as the woman, created society.

MINDY. "Created society?"

BARRY. Yeah, you gave birth to it. *We* can't give birth. *You* are the birth givers. *You*, metaphorically, birthed me. So, shame on *you* for how I turned out.

MINDY. I thought you wanted to win me back.

BARRY. *(whispering to CARL and PEGGY)* I'm trying reverse psychology.

MINDY. Can we please get back to the telethon?

CARL. Mindy's right. And so is Barry. It's not about us being together again. Yet, it is. It's about saving the station. Or *not* saving it. And it's about second chances. How many times do we get a second chance in life? Peggy?

PEGGY. *(catching her off guard)* Four?…

(Everyone looks at her.)

Five?

CARL. Not many. And this is our chance to show our beloved fans in…

(He draws a blank, then looks back at the sign.)

MINDY. Maple Valley.

CARL. …That we are bigger than this. We coulda had class. We coulda been a contender…And this is our chance to save WKLN with our totally awesome musical stylings so we can tour like Mindy promised.

MINDY. Yeah, I don't think that's gonna happen, now.

CARL. Not even a neck brace will prevent me from entertaining 'em.

(He takes off his neck brace, and feels a sharp pain.)

Ohh, daggers…So, what do you say? Let's get a second wind, shake things up, and make some money for WKLN!

(LANCE enters with the Scotch.)

LANCE. I can't believe it. We just lost two hundred dollars after that last song. What the heck is going on, here!?

(He moves the thermometer down to 1,300.)

STATION MANAGER. *(V.O.)* And we're live in three, two, one.

*(**LANCE** sets the Scotch offstage as the "On Air" light turns on. Everyone smiles.)*

LANCE. *(into mic)* Hellooooo.

PEGGY. Lance, there's only one thing we can do right now. And that's bump our booty rump.

LANCE. Wait, that's a happy song. They don't like happy songs.

*(**PEGGY** looks up to Todd and nods. The music starts.)*

(groans)

Ohh.

EVERYONE. *(sings)*
BUMP, BUMP, BUMP YOUR BOOTY RUMP.
BUMP, BUMP, BUMP YOUR BOOTY RUMP.

PEGGY & MINDY.
WHEN YOU'RE FEELIN' DOWN AND BLUE,
AND YOU DON'T KNOW WHAT TO DO.
YOU JUST FIND A RUMP,
AND YOU DO THE BUMP,
IT'LL MAKE YOU FEEL BRAND NEW.

EVERYONE.
BUMP, BUMP, BUMP YOUR BOOTY RUMP.
BUMP, BUMP, BUMP YOUR BOOTY RUMP.

BUMP IT HIGH,
YOU CAN BUMP IT LOW,
YOU CAN BUMP YOUR THIGH,
BUMP YOUR LITTLE TOE.

BUMP ALL DAY,
THEN YOU BUMP SOME MORE,
BUMP THE BLUES AWAY,
OR TIL YOUR RUMP IS SORE.

BUMP, BUMP, BUMP YOUR BOOTY RUMP.
BUMP, BUMP, BUMP YOUR BOOTY RUMP.

MINDY.

WHEN YOUR MAN HAS DONE YOU WRONG,

(**BARRY** *looks at* **MINDY.**)

AND YOU DON'T FEEL VERY STRONG,

BARRY. *(to* **MINDY**) Those aren't the lyrics.

MINDY.

DON'T YOU POUT AND DON'T YOU GROUSE,
KICK HIM OUT AND TAKE THE HOUSE,
THEN BUMP YOUR RUMP.

EVERYONE.

BUMP, BUMP, BUMP YOUR BOOTY RUMP.

MINDY.

TAKE THE CAR.

EVERYONE.

BUMP, BUMP, BUMP YOUR BOOTY RUMP.

MINDY.

TAKE THE POODLE.

EVERYONE.

BUMP, BUMP, BUMP YOUR BOOTY RUMP.

MINDY.

GO TO PARIS.

EVERYONE.

BUMP, BUMP, BUMP YOUR BOOTY RUMP.

MINDY.

GET A BOOB JOB.

EVERYONE.

BUMP, BUMP, BUMP YOUR BOOTY RUMP.

MINDY.

BUY A MONKEY.

EVERYONE.

BUMP YOUR BOOTY RUMP.

LANCE. *(He reaches offstage and grabs a note card. He then takes a sip of Scotch, then sets it offstage.)* Alright! Fantastic! We just got in four hundred dollars from the Maple Valley Chiropractic Clinic.

(He moves the thermometer up to $1,700.)

CARL.   **PEGGY.**

Awesome!   Sweet!

LANCE. We are back! Now, if you pledge three hundred dollars, you will receive Carl's Nepalese cookbook, "Curry on a Sherpa Budget." Tell 'em what else they'll get, Erma.

(The "On Air" light goes off.)

STATION MANAGER. *(V.O.)* And we're out.

(Everyone relaxes. **LANCE** *exits.)*

BARRY. *(to* **MINDY***)* Yeah, I don't remember writing those lyrics.

MINDY. *(smiling)* Yeah, I improvised a little.

BARRY. Are you actually smiling?

MINDY. *(She stops smiling.)* No.

BARRY. I have an announcement.

MINDY. Oh, great.

BARRY. I asked our manager to go ahead and book a reunion tour for us. We have 32 performance dates already lined up.

CARL.   **PEGGY.**

Right on!   Yes!

BARRY. We just have to make it thru this telethon without destroying the station to lock 'em in.

MINDY. That's a little presumptuous, isn't it?

BARRY. You said if we make ten thousand dollars for the station we can tour.

MINDY. Yeah, I said that like a half hour ago, before you cheated on me, twice, that I know about.

BARRY. We go on tour, do the old stuff, maybe work in some new material. A new sound.

CARL. *(concerned)* A new sound?

MINDY. We don't need a new sound.

BARRY. Yes, we do.

CARL. *(concerned)* Why?

MINDY. Yeah, why?

BARRY. Because disco *sucks*!

CARL. *(cries)* Ohhh.

> *(**PEGGY** consoles **CARL**.)*

MINDY. Okay, you have said some hurtful things in your day but that really takes the cake.

BARRY. Disco is *dead*!

CARL. *(cries)* Oh, god, no!!

> *(**PEGGY** consoles **CARL**.)*

MINDY. It is not!

BARRY. Disco died on July 12th, 1979, at Comiskey Park when they burned all those disco records.

MINDY. Don't you dare say that, mister!

BARRY. No one has worn polyester for 20 years. I think it causes cancer.

CARL. That explains my vestigial tail.

MINDY. Alright, listen! We're gonna make that ten thousand dollars, they're gonna build that Disco Hall of Fame, we're gonna be immortalized, and disco is gonna live forever!

BARRY. See? You *do* care.

MINDY. What?

BARRY. You care about disco. It means something to you.

MINDY. You were messin' with me. Don't you mess with me!

BARRY. What is it gonna take to get you to tour again?

MINDY. I want you to grovel.

BARRY. I have been groveling!

MINDY. Grovel more.

BARRY. *(thinks)* Okay, you know what? We don't need you, anyway. You're not so special.

> *(to **CARL** and **PEGGY**)*

We'll just go on tour, just the three of us.

CARL. *(whispers to **PEGGY**)* Reverse psychology.

MINDY. Alright, fine.

(*She starts to leave.*)

CARL. *(whispers to* **PEGGY***)* It worked in reverse.

BARRY. Will you come back here.

MINDY. *(She stops and turns back.)* If you don't need me why do you want me to come back?

BARRY. Because I love you. It's why I'm here.

MINDY. Okay, so…you insult me, and then you say you love me?

BARRY. *(thinks)* It's tough love.

STATION MANAGER. *(V.O.)* And we're live in three, two, one.

(*The "On Air" light goes on.* **LANCE** *enters with the Scotch. Everyone smiles.*)

LANCE. Live, live, live, blah, blah, blah…

BARRY. …Lance, we'd like to do a song about what we were just talking about.

LANCE. Okay.

(**BARRY** *nods to Todd. The music starts.* **LANCE** *exits.*)

EVERYONE. *(sings)*
 TOUGH LOVE, TOUGH LOVE,
 TOUGH LOVE, TOUGH LOVE.
BARRY & MINDY.
 WHY CAN'T LOVE BE EASIER, THAN IT IS?
 WHY IS LOVE MUCH SLEAZIER, IN SHOWBIZ?
MINDY.
 I NEED SOMEONE WHO'LL LOVE ME SO MUCH, SO MUCH
  LESS CHEESIER
 THAN YOU HAD LOVED ME ONCE BEFORE.
EVERYONE.
 TOUGH LOVE.
 I NEED SOMEONE TO LOVE ME NOW.
 TOUGH LOVE.
 LOVE ME, FOR WHO I AM.
 TOUGH LOVE.
 I NEED SOMEONE TO TAKE THE VOW.
 TOUGH LOVE. IT'S TOUGH.

BARRY.

IT'S SO VERY TOUGH TO LOVE.

EVERYONE.

TOUGH LOVE, TOUGH LOVE,
TOUGH LOVE, TOUGH LOVE.

MINDY.

I DON'T KNOW WHY YOU TREATED ME WITH DISRESPECT,

(**BARRY** *shrugs, "I don't know."*)

DON'T YOU TRY TO PLEAD THE FIFTH, I
DO SUSPECT THAT YOU WILL
NEED TOUGH LOVIN' SO YOU'LL
LEARN YOUR LESSON IF YOU
WANT TO GET BACK IN THE DOOR.

EVERYONE.

TOUGH LOVE.
I NEED SOMEONE TO LOVE ME NOW.
TOUGH LOVE.
LOVE ME, FOR WHO I AM.
TOUGH LOVE. I NEED SOMEONE TO TAKE THE VOW.
TOUGH LOVE. IT'S TOUGH.

BARRY.

IT'S SO VERY TOUGH TO LOVE.

EVERYONE.

TOUGH LOVE, TOUGH LOVE,
TOUGH LOVE, TOUGH LOVE. TOUGH LOVE.

LANCE. *(entering, holding a note card)* Tough love. Reminds me of when my parents sent me to camp for the summer, and when I came home…they'd moved.

(He cries.)

Why!?…Mother!…

(looking offstage, collecting himself)

What?…Read the card?

(reading the note card)

Okay, we got another pledge, here. Three hundred dollars from Lucy's Dating Service, "where they make

LANCE. *(cont.)* love easy and affordable. There's no tough love at Lucy's, unless you pay for it…and for an extra fifty dollars you can get the full…

STATION MANAGER. *(V.O.)* *(cutting him off)* …And we're out.

(The "On Air" light goes out. (Everyone relaxes.)

LANCE. *(moving up the thermometer to $2,000, looking offstage)* You can do it, guys. I know you can.

(As he exits, he mutters to himself.)

We are so screwed.

BARRY. *(to MINDY)* You gotta admit, we work well together.

MINDY. Yeah, when we're fighting. It's the only time they like us.

BARRY. That's what people are into these days, fighting on dysfunctional talk shows.

MINDY. Yeah, well, I liked the old days, better.

CARL. Cause the old days were happier with disco. And it's our responsibility to bring disco back to save the world, and make it a happy place again.

PEGGY. With a Disco Hall of Fame.

CARL. Where they'll name a sandwich after us.

MINDY. *(to BARRY)* Why do you wanna tour so badly? I mean, you don't need the money. You have "Better Together." I'm sure you make good royalties from it. Why don't you just retire to the Bahamas or something?

BARRY. I lost "Better Together."

CARL.	**PEGGY.**
What?	What?

MINDY. You what?

BARRY. After we broke up, I went to Reno to play some of the clubs. I met a blackjack dealer named "Ureetha." I moved in with her, got hooked on gambling, and I lost the publishing rights to "Better Together" in a poker game.

MINDY. How could you do that?!

BARRY. I had a full house!

MINDY. You lost the rights to the only song that really meant anything to this group?

BARRY. If it means so much, why don't you wanna sing it?

MINDY. *(realizing something)* Oh, my gosh.

BARRY. What?

MINDY. It wasn't about love, was it?

BARRY. What wasn't about love?

MINDY. Why you came back.

BARRY. What?

MINDY. You don't wanna get back together because you love me. You wanna get back together because you're broke.

BARRY. That's not true. Entirely.

MINDY. You're here for the money!

BARRY. Hey, I am not the bad guy, here, okay?…It's *society*!…

MINDY. …Oh, jeez. You're using us. Conning us to get back together so you can continue your gambling addiction.

BARRY. *(sarcastic)* Thanks for the empathy. And my therapist thanks you, too.

MINDY. *(to BARRY)* User!

BARRY. Okay, let's not resort to name calling.

MINDY. You're weak!

CARL & PEGGY. *(reacting to the insult)* Oooh.

BARRY. You're over-rated!

CARL & PEGGY. Aaahh.

MINDY. Your lyrics sound like Mickey Mouse on crack!

CARL & PEGGY. Ohhh.

BARRY. When I hear you sing, my ears wanna vomit!

CARL & PEGGY. Eeewe.

MINDY. You sing like a cat choking on a hair ball!

(She mimics a cat choking on a hair ball.)

CARL & PEGGY. Oooh.

(**LANCE** *enters with his Scotch.*)

LANCE. I know that song.

(*He sets the Scotch offstage.*)

STATION MANAGER. *(V.O.)* And we're live in three, two, one.

(*The "On Air" sign goes on. Everyone smiles.*)

LANCE. *(into mic)* I'm single, I like long walks on the beach and playing Mah Jong. Call me.

MINDY. Lance, I'd like to do a song about feelings.

(*She looks up to Todd and nods.*)

LANCE. (*He sings the first two notes of the Morris Albert song, "Feelings."*)
FEELINGS!

(*The music starts, cutting him off.*)

EVERYONE. *(singing, forcing a smile)*
YOU YANK MY CHAIN,
YOU MAKE ME GO INSANE.
YOU YANK MY CHAIN...
MINDY.
WHEN YOU SAY THOSE THINGS TO ME.
BARRY.
THOSE ROTTEN THINGS THAT YOU SAY TO ME.
MINDY.
I WANNA SCREAM AND SHOUT,
BARRY.
I WANNA WRING YOU OUT,
MINDY.
I WANNA SHAKE YOU LIKE A TREE.
BARRY.
YOU WERE NICE TO ME LONG AGO.
MINDY.
YOU RAISED ME UP TO A NEW PLATEAU.
BARRY.
AND NOW I'M IN A TROUGH,

MINDY.

AND THE GLOVES ARE OFF,
I HOPE YOU HAVE A GOOD H.M.O.

EVERYONE.

YOU YANK MY CHAIN.
YOU MAKE ME GO INSANE.
YOU YANK MY CHAIN.

*(**NOTE:** Each actor sings a letter individually [Y-A-N-K-M-Y-C-H-A-I-N] then all together on "YANK, YANK.")*

Y-A-N-K-M-Y-C-H-A-I-N, YANK, YANK.
Y-A-N-K-M-Y-C-H-A-I-N, YANK, YANK.

CARL & PEGGY.

YOU YANK MY CHAIN, YOU YANK MY CHAIN,

BARRY & MINDY.

MY ANGER I WILL NOT CONTAIN.

CARL & PEGGY.

YOU YANK MY CHAIN, YOU YANK MY CHAIN,

BARRY & MINDY.

I'LL SPIN YOU LIKE A WEATHER VANE.

CARL.

THE GOLDEN RULE SAYS YOU SHOULD BE NICE.
BEFORE YOU ACT YOU SHOULD BOTH THINK TWICE.

MINDY.

AND IF YOUR CHEEK IS TURNED,
AND YOU STILL GET BURNED,
STICK HIS HEAD IN A WOODEN VICE.

EVERYONE.

YOU YANK MY CHAIN.
YOU MAKE ME GO INSANE.
YOU YANK MY CHAIN.

*(**NOTE:** Each actor sings a letter individually [Y-A-N-K-M-Y-C-H-A-I-N] then all together on "YANK, YANK.")*

Y-A-N-K-M-Y-C-H-A-I-N, YANK, YANK.
Y-A-N-K-M-Y-C-H-A-I-N, YANK, YANK.

BARRY & MINDY.

YOU YANK MY CHAIN, YOU YANK MY CHAIN,

CARL & PEGGY.

I'LL HIT YOU LIKE A CHOO CHOO TRAIN.

BARRY & MINDY.

YOU YANK MY CHAIN, YOU YANK MY CHAIN,

CARL & PEGGY.

I'LL AMPUTATE YOUR LITTLE BRAIN.

EVERYONE.

YOU YANK MY CHAIN.

YOU YANK MY CHAIN.

YOU YANK MY CHAIN.

LANCE. *(grabbing a few cards from offstage)* Fantastic! Wow! The pledges are comin in, folks. We just…

(reading a note card)

We just doubled our money! Here's one of the pledges from Margaret Henderson for two hundred dollars. Margaret has a request, she would like to "yank Barry's chain."

(He laughs.)

Who wouldn't?

(He moves the thermometer up to $4,000.)

We just need another six thousand dollars to keep our doors open. Seems like a lot. It is. So all you kids at home, open your mom's purse, get her credit card and call us so we can continue to provide you with quality programming such as,

(reading from the note card)

"The Use of Dried Raisins in Food Planning."

(looks offstage)

Really?

(The "On Air" light goes off.)

STATION MANAGER. *(V.O.)* And we're out.

(Everyone relaxes.)

BARRY. Hey, Lance, what about selling copies of this video tape?

(holding up the tape)

I bet that would bring in some money.

LANCE. No, no, no. That's a collector's item. Copies would just diminish the value. We'll get there. Don't worry.

(as he exits with the Scotch, looking offstage)

I need a refill.

CARL. This is awesome! We're making progress, and that's what it's all about. Healing. And everyone has a different way to heal. You know how they heal people in New Guinea?…

(He waits a beat for an answer.)

I don't know, I'm just askin'.

PEGGY. Carl, I think it's really sweet that you're trying so hard to get us back together.

CARL. That's what it's all about, girlfriend. Getting back together. And organic farming. Did you know you can grow mushrooms in a totally dark room with just poop.

BARRY. Carl, focus.

CARL. Right.

(collecting himself)

So, what do you wanna sing next?

MINDY. You know, what's the point? Really. The only serious pledges we get are when we're fighting, and we only have a couple more "fight" songs left. I mean, the only way we're gonna hit ten thousand dollars is if we have a Jerry Springer chair brawl.

BARRY. Hey, don't go all despondent on us. If we have love we can do anything.

MINDY. Oh, give it a rest.

CARL. This is good. They're making up.

PEGGY. It doesn't seem like it.

CARL. But they are. You see, what's the opposite of love? Peggy?

PEGGY. *(catching her off guard)* Car wash? No wait, jury duty. No, chicken pox! That's it! Chicken pox!

CARL. *(taking that in for a beat)* Most people say hate. But that's not true. The opposite of love is indifference.

PEGGY. I hate pop quizzes.

CARL. *(to* **BARRY** *and* **MINDY***)* There's a fine line between love and hate, and right now you two are playin' tug of war, like a French mime in spandex.

(He starts playing tug of war like a mime, then mimes being trapped in a box.)

There isn't enough love in the world, and what little love there is, people want it to go away…What was I talkin' about?

PEGGY. Love?

CARL. They want love to die. But we won't let it. No. Cause we're gonna fight to get love back.

MINDY. *(giving in)* Yeah, maybe Carl's right.

CARL. I am?

BARRY. So…I have a chance?

MINDY. You know what you have to do.

CARL & PEGGY. *(chanting)* Grovel, grovel, grovel, grovel…

STATION MANAGER. *(V.O.)*…And we're live in three, two, one.

(The "On Air" light goes on. **LANCE** *steps back on stage with the Scotch. Everyone smiles.)*

LANCE. *(Into mic. A bit more drunk.)* Houston, we have a problem.

(He laughs.)

MINDY. *(to the camera)* Lance, I have a confession to make.

LANCE. Mindy has a confession!

(puts his finger to his lips)

Shhhh!

MINDY. I didn't sleep with Carl.

CARL. I *knew* it!

BARRY. Yes!

LANCE. Now, *this* is good television!

MINDY. Oh, and one more thing. Barry wets the bed.

BARRY. *(to* **MINDY***)* I was drunk!

MINDY. What are you gonna do? Throw a chair?! Throw it!! Throw it!!

(She turns and winks at **CARL.***)*

LANCE. *(handing* **BARRY** *a stool)* What is it, sweeps week?!

CARL. Stand back, Lance. It's a war on love!

(He looks up to the booth and nods to Todd.)

(The music starts.)

(sings)

THERE'S A WAR A BREWIN' OUT THERE.
A WAR ON LOVE IS DE-CLARED.
ATTACKIN' LOVE AFFAIRS IS UNFAIR.
BECAUSE TRUE LOVE IS SO RARE.

WE GOTTA FIGHT FOR THE RIGHT TO LOVE RIGHT NOW.
THERE'S A WAR AGAINST LOVE,
WE GOTTA STOP IT, AND I KNOW HOW.

I'M GONNA GO TO WAR,
GONNA FIGHT FOR LOVE.
GONNA WEAR MY "LOVE HURTS" BOXING GLOVE,
GONNA DROP A LOVE BOMB FROM ABOVE.
GONNA SHOOT MY LOVE GUN…
GONNA AIM FOR LOVE.

(riffing)

I'm a good shot, too. I can hit love. Like, you put love in front of me and I will hit it.

(continues to sing)

THE ENEMY IS RIGHT THERE.
WE GOT LOVE TANKS EVERYWHERE.
I GOT YOU IN MY CROSS HAIR.
SURRENDER OR BEWARE.

CARL. *(cont.)*

I'M GONNA FIGHT FOR THE RIGHT FOR YOUR EMBRACE,
I'M GONNA TOSS MY LOVE GRENADE,
ON YOUR FACE.

I'M GONNA GO TO WAR,
GONNA FIGHT FOR LOVE.
CAUSE YOU'RE THE ONLY ONE I AM THINKING OF.
GONNA DROP A LOVE BOMB FROM ABOVE,
GONNA SHOOT MY LOVE GUN.
GONNA AIM FOR LOVE.

(riffing over the end music)

We're gonna fight for love. We're gonna get these two together if it kills us. We'll send in the love beret. We're gonna have explosions of love, and casualties of love, and we're gonna call in the Salvation Army of Love. We're gonna fight for love! Fight for it! Fight for love!

(The song ends, a la Elvis.)

Thank you. Thank you very much.

LANCE. *(reaching offstage for a card)* The phone is ringin' off the hook, folks. Here's a pledge that just came in for…

(reading the card)

three hundred dollars from the National Rifle Association.

CARL. Rifle man!

LANCE. *(He moves the thermometer up to $6,000.)* You are lookin' at the next Channel 9 anchorman!

(Looking offstage. Defiantly.)

What?…I don't need any coffee!…

(He exits with the Scotch. The "On Air" light goes off.)

STATION MANAGER. *(V.O.)* And we're out.

(Everyone relaxes.)

CARL. I am stoked!

PEGGY. How do you do it, Carl? How can you be so optimistic all the time?

CARL. It's easy. Because of you. I mean, you're such a beacon of hope. You're so real and honest...

PEGGY. ...I don't teach drivers' training...

CARL. ...YOU'RE A LIAR!

PEGGY. *(cries)* Ohh.

BARRY. You don't teach driver's training?

PEGGY. No.

CARL. *(cries)* Oh, just kill me.

MINDY. *(to* **CARL***)* What happened to optimism?

CARL. I'm a fake, alright. I can barely hold it together. The only thing real about me is my polyester pants, that, although highly flammable, I don't have to iron.

MINDY. So, if you're not a driver's training instructor, what are you?

PEGGY. Well...umm...okay, so, when our group broke up, I just needed to get away, right. So...I moved to Florida and became a Hooters Girl.

BARRY. You're a Hooters Girl?

PEGGY. I was.

CARL. Why did you say you were a driver's training instructor?

PEGGY. Because I thought you would respect me more if I taught drivers' training rather than dressing up in a skimpy outfit and serving chicken wings to horny guys.

CARL. *(thinks)* Not really.

PEGGY. I mean the tips were good and everything and the customers liked me, but then one day someone asked me if I would consider stripping.

BARRY. Awesome!...

MINDY. (**MINDY** *shoots him a look.*) ...Barry...

BARRY. *(He quickly reverses his tone, to* **PEGGY***)* ...That's terrible.

PEGGY. And I realized I didn't wanna end up being a stripper. I wanted to be respected for my talent, and not for my...you know.

(motioning to her breasts with cupped hands)

CARL. Arthritis?

PEGGY. That was the day I knew I had to quit.

CARL. That was so brave of you.

PEGGY. And I'm not dating anyone.

CARL. *(hopeful)* You're not?

PEGGY. I'm a terrible person.

> *(cries)*

CARL. Oh, no, you're not. You're just a liar.

PEGGY. *(cries)* Ohhh.

CARL. I didn't mean that in a bad way.

BARRY. So…do you really have a son?

PEGGY. Yes, I have a son! I'm not a liar! I mean, okay, except for saying I taught drivers' training…and the part about *not* stripping.

BARRY. *(enthusiastic)* I knew it!…

MINDY. …Barry…

BARRY. *(quickly to **PEGGY**)* …You do not need to strip.

PEGGY. I don't anymore, okay. I quit, like, five da…

> *(corrects herself)*

years ago.

MINDY. Why would you even do that?

PEGGY. I don't know, it's just that…I wanted to feel what it was like to be *you.*

MINDY. Honey, I was never a stripper.

PEGGY. Well, not technically…I'm talking about all the attention you got. I wanted that same feeling.

MINDY. Is that why you slept with Barry? To see what it was like to be me?

PEGGY. I am so sorry. I don't know what I was thinking. Barry is such an idiot!

BARRY. Hellooo.

PEGGY. I don't know, it was just always so hard being in your shadow.

MINDY. Me? In my shadow?

PEGGY. Well, yeah. I mean, *you're* the group. No offense, Barry. But people came to see *you*. People loved you, and I just…I don't know, I wanted to feel what it was like to be in the limelight, you know…to shine.

MINDY. Well, why didn't you say anything?

CARL. I still wanna marry you even though thousands of men have seen your Virginia.

PEGGY. *(smiling, encouraged)* You do?

CARL. Yeah.

(leans in close as if to kiss her, then stops)

Your mascara really makes your eyes pop.

STATION MANAGER. *(V.O.)* And we're live in three, two, one.

(The "On Air" sign goes on. LANCE enters with the Scotch. Everyone smiles.)

LANCE. *(to the camera)* I declare today, "National Disco Day!"

PEGGY. Lance, I'd like to do a song I wrote that I've never done in public. It's for everyone out there who would like to shine.

(She nods to Todd.)

LANCE. I'm shinin' right now.

(The music starts. CARL and MINDY look at each other like they don't know the song. NOTE: PEGGY starts off shy and by the end of the song she has completely come out of her shell.)

PEGGY. *(sings)*
I'M IN THE SHADOWS OF THE SPOTLIGHT,
A DARK CORNER OF THE STAGE.
IN THE SECOND ROW, WHERE THE LIGHTS ARE LOW,
LIKE A GROUNDHOG IN A CAGE.

WHERE I'M KEPT ALL DAY IN DARKNESS,
BY THE KEEPER OF THE ZOO.
WISHIN' EVERY DAY, I COULD RUN AWAY,
I WOULD BID THIS CAGE ADIEU,
I don't need no stinkin' Groundhog Day.
RUN, GROUNDHOG, RUN,
TAKE A CHANCE IN LIFE AND TURN THE PAGE.

CARL.

RUN, GROUNDHOG, RUN,

(encouraging **BARRY** *and* **MINDY** *to join in)*

PEGGY.

THRU THE TRAP DOOR, AND ESCAPE THE CAGE.

CARL & MINDY & BARRY.

RUN, GROUNDHOG, RUN,

PEGGY.

TO THE LIGHT AND TAKE THE CENTER STAGE.

CARL & MINDY & BARRY.

RUN, GROUNDHOG.

PEGGY.

TO THE LIGHT AND TAKE THE STAGE.

CARL. *(to* **MINDY***)* Oh, it's a story about a groundhog.

MINDY. It's a metaphor, doofus.

CARL. *(I see.)* Oh, a metaphor…

(No, I don't.)

Yeah, I don't know what that is.

PEGGY.

ALL MY LIFE I'VE BEEN A GROUNDHOG,
WAITIN' FOR MY DAY TO SHINE.
ALL MY WORK IS NAUGHT, I'M A SECOND THOUGHT,
ALL I DO IS TOE THE LINE.

I DON'T GET NO SATISFACTION,
SEEIN' DAYLIGHT ONCE A YEAR.
GONNA TAKE A CHANCE, GONNA SING AND DANCE.
ALL THE KIDS ARE GONNA CHEER,
"Mommy, the groundhog is escaping!"

CARL & MINDY & BARRY.

RUN, GROUNDHOG, RUN,

PEGGY.

PAST THE ZOO KEEPER AND FLEE THE CAGE.

CARL & MINDY & BARRY.

RUN, GROUNDHOG, RUN,

PEGGY.

NO MORE GROUNDHOG I HAVE COME OF AGE.

CARL & MINDY & BARRY.

RUN, PEGGY, RUN,

PEGGY. *(taking centerstage)*

TO THE LIGHT AND TAKE THE CENTERSTAGE.

CARL & MINDY & BARRY.

SHINE, PEGGY.

PEGGY.

I'M IN THE LIGHT ON CENTERSTAGE.

EVERYONE.

SHINE, PEGGY, SHINE.

SHINE, PEGGY, SHINE.

LANCE. *(reaching offstage for a card)* Fantastic! We just received two hundred dollars from the Maple Valley Petting Zoo.

(He moves the thermometer up to $6,500.)

PEGGY. Yes!

CARL. Remember to spay or neuter your groundhog!

(The "On Air" light goes off.)

STATION MANAGER. *(V.O.)*…And we're out.

(Everyone relaxes. LANCE exits.)

MINDY. So…you're the groundhog?

PEGGY. Uh huh.

MINDY. And I'm the…?

CARL. …The zoo keeper. See, I'm following this.

MINDY. Okay, thank you…Gosh, I just…Hon, I didn't realize how selfish I've been.

PEGGY. Oh, don't beat yourself up. I have another kidney.

MINDY. *(to BARRY, CARL & PEGGY)* Why don't you three do the tour without me?

BARRY. Who will I sing "Mindy's Song" to?

MINDY. Sing it to Peggy. She deserves the limelight. She can be the new front person.

BARRY. We need you.

MINDY. No, you don't…You were right. I *did* think I was special, okay. But I'm not.

BARRY. Yes, you are! Look, I'm sorry I said that, alright. You *are* special.

(**LANCE** *enters with the Scotch.*)

STATION MANAGER. *(V.O.)* And we're live in three, two, one.

(*The "On Air" light turns on. Everyone smiles.*)

LANCE. We just got a pledge of one thousand dollars from Carl's mom!

(*He moves up the thermometer to $7,500.*)

CARL. *(giving a victory arm pump)* Yes!

LANCE. Apparently she wants Carl outta the house.

CARL. *(holding back tears)* Thanks, Mom.

LANCE. Which brings us up to seven thousand, five hundred, twenty-four dollars and twelve donuts! Come on, people, just twenty-five hundred more and we'll all be eatin' a Synchronistics Club Sandwich in the ABBA Cafeteria!

PEGGY. Just down the hall from the Bee Gees wing, right next to the Travolta John…

(*Everyone looks at her.*)

I saw the plans.

BARRY. Lance, I'd like to do a song I wrote about someone very special.

(*to* **MINDY**)

Mindy.

(*He nods to Todd.*)

LANCE. Oh, I love this song!

(*The music starts.*)

CARL. Oh, he's gonna do "Mindy's Song." Good one, Barry.

PEGGY. Carl, let 'em have their moment.

CARL. *(waves his hand in front of his face, whispering)* Cloak on.

BARRY. *(sings)*

> SOME ONE VERY SPECIAL,
> CAME IN TO MY HEART.
> SOON SHE TOOK MY WORLD APART.
> LOVING, CARING, MORE THAN SHE COULD KNOW.
> I LOVE HER SO.

> WHEREVER I GO,
> I ALWAYS THINK OF MINDY.

CARL & PEGGY.

> MINDY.

BARRY.

> MY LIFE IS AGLOW,
> WHEN I'M WITH THAT GIRL.

CARL & PEGGY.

> THAT GIRL.

BARRY.

> SHE'S THE SWEETEST GIRL I KNOW.
> OH, MINDY, GIRL. HOW I LOVE YOU SO.

CARL & PEGGY.

> LOVE YOU SO.

BARRY.

> LIGHT OF MY SOUL,

MINDY. How do I know?

BARRY.

> YOU MAKE ME WHOLE.

MINDY. Do you really mean that?

BARRY.

> DON'T LET ME GO.

MINDY. Why should I stay?

BARRY.

> I LOVE YOU SO.

MINDY. You *say* that.

BARRY.

> WHEN I LOOK AROUND,
> ALL I SEE IS

BARRY.	**MINDY.**
MINDY.	ACTIONS DO SPEAK LOUDER THAN WORDS.

BARRY.

MY LIFE TURNED AROUND,
THE DAY I MET THAT

BARRY.	**MINDY.**
GIRL.	I WANT SO MUCH TO BELIEVE YOU.
SHE'S THE ONE	YOU SAY THESE THINGS,
WHO'S MEANT FOR ME.	BUT THEY'RE ONLY WORDS TO ME NOW.

BARRY.

OH, MINDY GIRL,

BARRY.	**MINDY.**
PLEASE BE WITH ME.	PLEASE STOP NOW.

BARRY.

OH, MINDY, GIRL, YOU

BARRY.	**MINDY.**
MAKE ME HAPPY.	DON'T BREAK MY HEART.

BARRY.

OH, MINDY, GIRL. WILL YOU MARRY ME.

*(As the song ends, **BARRY** holds his hand out to **MINDY**. **MINDY** reaches over to take his hand, but, still guarded, she pulls it away before their hands touch.)*

LANCE. *(emotional)* It is no wonder that "Mindy's Song" is the most played elevator song in France.

(He looks offstage.)

What's this? Another pledge?

(He reaches offstage and grabs a note card.)

Alright!

(reading the card)

We just…lost fifteen hundred dollars after that last song.

BARRY. *(standing up)* Crap!

LANCE. Are you kidding me?! What do you have, coal for a heart?!

(He turns the card over.)

Oh, there's more.

(reading)

They just put a "For Sale" sign on the building. Everyone needs to clear out their stuff when we're done.

STATION MANAGER. *(V.O.)* And we're out.

(The "On Air" light goes off. Everyone relaxes. LANCE moves the thermometer down to $6,000, despondent, holding his Scotch.)

MINDY. *(despondent)* We don't have anymore "fight songs."

PEGGY. There goes the Disco Hall of Fame.

CARL. We failed Maple Valley…

(getting emotional)

We couldn't do it. We couldn't save the station.

BARRY. Come on, we're in this together, okay. And it's not over yet.

CARL. Hey, I have a thought.

MINDY. Oh, no.

CARL. What if, like, the station did shows that people actually wanted to watch, then maybe more people would watch. Just throwin' that out at ya.

MINDY. I'm sorry, Lance.

(She turns to leave.)

BARRY. Okay, that does it.

*(**BARRY** grabs the VCR video tape copy of their first performance on WKLN, from the table.)*

LANCE. Hey!

BARRY. *(holding the video)* Mindy, if you don't come back and finish the telethon, I'll destroy the video.

*(**MINDY** stops and turns back.)*

LANCE. *(cries)* Ohhh!

PEGGY. Oh, my gosh.

BARRY. Which will destroy the only memory of our start here in Maple Valley.

LANCE. *(emotional)* Don't let him do it!

CARL. Come on, man, you're holding our entire world in your hand…

(taking two steps toward BARRY*)*

BARRY. …Stand back or I'll smash it to pieces!

(He lifts the video above his head. CARL *steps back.)*

LANCE. *(emotional)* Please don't break it! That video means everything to me. It's priceless.

BARRY. I can get ya five thousand dollars for it.

LANCE. Sold!

*(*LANCE *casually exits.)*

CARL. Step away from the video!…Come on, man, put it down. Gently. On the floor. No one will get hurt.

PEGGY. Don't throw it all away, Barry. Or at least put me in your will, first.

CARL. *(to* BARRY*)* Think about your ex-con prison man-baby!…Come on, Mindy. Stop him.

MINDY. *(thinks)* Go ahead and destroy it.

PEGGY. Oh, no.

CARL. Don't do it, Barry!

BARRY. I'm not bluffing.

MINDY. Fine. If our past doesn't mean anything to you, go ahead and smash it to pieces.

CARL. *(chanting)* HARI KRISHNA, HARI KRISHNA, HARI RAMA, HARI RAMA, RAMA RAMA, KRISHNA KRISHNA, HARI HARI…

(continues chanting under his breath)

*(*BARRY *thinks for a few moments, then puts the video down on the table.* CARL *stops chanting.)*

(amazed) It worked!

BARRY. I can't do it…Look, I'll have our manager cancel the tour. I'm sorry I booked it.

CARL. *(groans)* Ohh, it's like gettin' punched by Apollo Creed.

*(*BARRY *starts to walk away.)*

PEGGY. Okay, you win. I'm sorry.

BARRY. *(He stops and turns back.)* What are *you* sorry about?

PEGGY. Okay, well, first, I just wanna say it's been really good seeing everyone again.

CARL. I love you, now, more than I ever have.

PEGGY. I lied about the Disco Hall of Fame.

CARL. I DON'T EVEN KNOW YOU!

PEGGY. I was the one who told our manager they were breaking ground on the Disco Hall of Fame, and that we would be inducted, when really they were just voting on whether to build it. And I told him this telethon was part of the deal to help publicize it.

MINDY. Why did you lie about it?

PEGGY. Cause I thought it was the only thing that would get you to come back, and I wanted everyone here so I could say that I'm sorry, in person...It was my fault we broke up, okay, for sleeping with...

(looks at **BARRY***)*

BARRY. ...No it wasn't, Peggy, it was *my* fault.

PEGGY. *I* know. But *I* should have known better. Look, I just wanted to say how sorry I am to everyone for what I did. I mean, we had such a great thing together. We really did. And I've never been happier in my life than I was when we were together.

CARL. Me, too.

BARRY. Yeah, me, too.

PEGGY. *(emotional)* And it's my fault. I destroyed the best thing that anyone could ever have...our friendship...I love you guys, and I miss you so much...I just...I just hope, some day, you can forgive me.

CARL. I forgive you.

BARRY. I forgive you, too.

*(***PEGGY*** *shoots a look at* ***BARRY***. He mouths, "What?")*

PEGGY. *(Tearfully, she looks at* **MINDY***.)* Mindy, I am so sorry.

MINDY. *(thinks)* Oh, honey, I can't stay mad at you.

(She hugs her.)

PEGGY. Thank you.

> (*to* **BARRY** *and* **MINDY**)

You know, I was kinda hoping there might be some chance that you two might get back together, you know, like the good old days. Cause you're really good together. You really are.

> (**BARRY** *and* **MINDY** *look at each other. They don't say anything.*)

Anyway…I'm just happy that Mindy came back.

BARRY. What about me?

PEGGY. You're here because you're broke and you want us to go back on tour. Mindy didn't have to come back.

> (*to* **MINDY**)

I know how busy you are with your solo career.

MINDY. Yeah, well, that's not entirely true.

CARL. What, are we all a bunch of *liars*?!

MINDY. I tried to tour, okay. After we split up, I tried to go out on my own. I played small clubs, weddings, but everywhere I went it was the same thing, "play 'Better Together,' play 'Mindy's Song.'" Well, you know what, it's kinda hard to sing a love song to yourself. And so I started losing confidence, and…

PEGGY. …Why?

MINDY. I don't know.

> (*mumbles to herself, inaudible*)

Becau I din hav arry er tehing…

PEGGY. I'm sorry, what?

MINDY. Because I didn't have Barry there telling me how great I was, okay? There, I said it.

> (*to* **BARRY**, *emotional*)

You gave me the confidence, you built me up to something I probably never was, and then you took it away… You took it away.

BARRY. I am so sorry.

MINDY. And so the gigs started drying up, and after awhile I couldn't even book a taxi. And you know why? Because they didn't want *me*, okay? They wanted *us*.

CARL. That's what it's all about! Don't you see? We do best when we're together. The sum of the parts is greater than the car after it's been stripped.

(LANCE enters with his Scotch.)

STATION MANAGER. *(V.O.)* And we're live in three, two, one.

(The "On Air" light goes on. Everyone smiles.)

LANCE. We have time for one more song, and then we can all go home and sell our organs.

(He looks offstage with his hand on his ear piece.)

What? I don't want any coffee!

(groans)

Ahh.

(He exits.)

CARL. We may be a dysfunctional family, okay, but we're "better together than we were apart"…

(He waits a beat for the music cue, but it doesn't come.)

We're "better together than we were apart"…

(Still waits, it doesn't come. He looks up to Todd.)

Todd, dude, that's, like, the music cue.

(The music starts.)

Kind of takes away from the moment, doesn't it?

PEGGY. That's okay. Things like that happen.

CARL. I mean, it's our *one hit*, and I'm tryin' to make a point that we work well together and…

BARRY. …Carl, focus.

CARL. Right.

(sings)

BEING ON MY OWN HAS HAD ITS PLUSES.
I'D SIT HOME WATCHING RE-RUNS OF KUNG FU.

BARRY & PEGGY & MINDY.

OOO OOO OOO.

MINDY.

LIFE CAN BE SO DIFFICULT WHEN YOU FACE IT ALL ALONE.

CARL.

GRASSHOPPER.

BARRY.

THE WORLD IS SO MUCH EASIER WITH YOU.

EVERYONE.

WE NEVER WERE AS GOOD APART AS WE WERE TOGETHER.

WE NEVER REALLY WERE AS SMART AS WE WERE TOGETHER.

WE TRIED IT ON OUR OWN.

AND WE SANK JUST LIKE A STONE.

NO MORE. DON'T WANT TO BE ALONE.

PEGGY.

SOMETIMES WHEN YOU'RE YOUNG YOU DON'T KNOW
    BETTER.

CARL.

ON THE ROAD I LEARNED A THING OR TWO.

BARRY & PEGGY & MINDY.

OOO OOO OOO.

MINDY.

THAT THE SUM OF ALL THE PARTS

IS SO MUCH GREATER THAN THE WHOLE.

BARRY.

I'M BETTER WHEN I AM NEXT TO YOU.

EVERYONE.

WE NEVER WERE AS GOOD APART AS WE WERE TOGETHER.

AND NOW I HAVE A BROKEN HEART AND I'M LOST FOREVER.

UNLESS WE CAN RENEW,

THE LOVE THAT WE ONCE KNEW.

I'M BETTER, WHEN I AM NEXT TO YOU.

BARRY.

I AM SO MUCH BETTER, WHEN I AM NEXT TO YOU.

(**LANCE** *enters, holding a cup of coffee.*)

LANCE. What did I miss?

(Puts his hand to his ear piece.)

I missed "Better Together?" Oh, crap! Can you play it again?

(He looks off.)

What?…This is my last telethon?…No kidding. This is *everyone's* last telethon.

(The "On Air" light goes off.)

STATION MANAGER. *(V.O.)* And we're out.

(Everyone relaxes.)

LANCE. Alright, guys. Let's go ahead and pack up our stuff. Thanks for tryin', everyone. I really appreciate it. Sorry it didn't work out.

BARRY. Okay, Lance, how much do we need to reach ten thousand dollars?

LANCE. Depends on how much we're gonna lose after that last song.

(looking offstage)

What?!…Okay. Four thousand dollars.

BARRY. Do they take Visa?

(taking his wallet out)

LANCE. If they take donuts, they'll take Visa.

BARRY. *(He hands* **LANCE** *his Visa card.)* Here, take the four thousand off that…Wait, make it an even ten thousand.

MINDY. Barry.

BARRY. This isn't gambling.

MINDY. Why are you doing this?

BARRY. We can't lose this station. It's where we got our start. It's part of our legacy. Besides, it might help our chances tomorrow when they vote on the Disco Hall of Fame.

MINDY. I thought you were broke.

BARRY. No. I make ten thousand dollars a month just on "Remember the Good Times We Had."

MINDY. *(gasping)* Ten thousand?

BARRY. Yeah, it does real well in Germany. I don't know.

LANCE. It's the theme song to the number one sitcom over there, "Rememberin' der Gooten Times-en, Yah."

MINDY. So...you didn't wanna get back together because you needed the money?

BARRY. No. Because I needed *you.*

PEGGY. Oh, that is so sweet.

BARRY. *(to* **MINDY***)* You said you lost confidence? You know how many songs I wrote while we were apart? None.

CARL. I thought you wrote that apology song.

BARRY. Technically, we were still together when I wrote that.

CARL. But not as a group.

BARRY. Carl, I'm tryin' to make a point, here...

CARL ...Go ahead.

BARRY. *(to* **MINDY***)* The point is, I haven't written a song in twenty years. Why? Because you are my muse. And I can't write when I'm not with you...You know how they say that "music is the lyric of the soul"...

CARL. ...Actually, music is the "*language*" of the soul...

BARRY. ...If you wreck this for me, Carl, I swear to god...

CARL. ...Go ahead.

BARRY. *(to* **MINDY***)* I have no soul when I'm not with you. You are a part of me.

CARL. Like John and Yoko.

BARRY. Carl!

CARL. *(waves his hand over his face)* Cloak on.

STATION MANAGER. *(V.O.)* And we're live in three, two, one.

(The "On Air" light goes on.)

LANCE. *(Seeing* **BARRY** *getting ready to confess to* **MINDY***, he whispers into mic.)* Welcome back.

BARRY. *(looks at the camera, then to* **MINDY***)* I love you, Mindy. And I know it might take awhile for me to win back your trust, but, I can wait, okay. So...what do you say

we, you know, hang out and maybe sing or somethin'
while I'm working to win you back?

(**MINDY** *smiles but doesn't respond.*)

PEGGY. I'm not doing it without you, Mindy.

CARL. I'm not either.

BARRY. We need you. *I* need you…You know what, I don't
even care if we go on tour.

CARL. *(groans)* Ohhh.

BARRY. I just want you back, alright, and I don't wanna go
another day without you. Look, I know I don't deserve
it, but if you give me another chance, I promise I won't
let you down.

CARL. *(to* **PEGGY***)* He just went "full grovel."

PEGGY. I think he's got one more.

BARRY. *(singing a capella)*

WE NEVER WERE AS GOOD APART AS WE WERE TOGETHER…

(Before he can continue, **MINDY** *cuts him off by kissing
him.)*

CARL. *(watching them kiss)* So…does this mean we're gonna
go on tour?

(He hears a muffled "Uh huh" from **MINDY** *as they continue to kiss.)*

Was that a "yes?"

MINDY. *(breaking from the kiss)* Yeah, we'll go on tour.

*(***BARRY*** smiles.)*

CARL & PEGGY. Yes!

*(***CARL*** and* **PEGGY** *hug.)*

LANCE. They're back together, folks! Live on WKLN! Is this
a great day, or what!

CARL. So, Barry, dude, you couldn't have, like, given' 'em
the ten thousand dollars, like, two hours ago?

BARRY. If I did that, do you think Mindy would have for-
given me?

CARL. No.

PEGGY. Not at all.

BARRY. So, Peggy, do you think your son would like to help us with the tour?

PEGGY. Yeah. That would be nice.

CARL. *(holding* **PEGGY***'s hands, looking into her eyes)* You are so beautiful.

PEGGY. Thank you, Carl.

CARL. *(moves closer)* Will you…let me move into your trailer with you?

PEGGY. *(smiling)* Sure.

LANCE. *(looking off)* It's official, folks! Barry's credit card went through! I knew we could do it! Pulitzer Prize baby! Disco Hall of Fame!

(The music starts. They all move to their mics.)

EVERYONE. *(sings)*
WE'RE TOGETHER AS FRIENDS, SINGIN' IN HARMONY.

BARRY & CARL.
ALL TOGETHER, SINGIN' ALL TOGETHER.

EVERYONE.
THE FOUR OF US IN SYNCHRONICITY.

BARRY & CARL.
ALL TOGETHER, FRIENDS WE'LL BE FOREVER.

BARRY & CARL.	**MINDY & PEGGY**
ANYTHING IS POSSIBLE.	OOOOOOH.
SET YOUR WORRIES	OOOOOOH.
FREE.	AAAAAH.

EVERYONE.
WHEN YOU'RE SINGIN' IN HARMONY.

PUT YOUR HANDS ON YOUR HIPS,
THEN TURN TO THE RIGHT.
THROW SOME COAL ON THE FIRE,
WE'LL BE DANCIN' ALL NIGHT.

ON THE FUNK TRAIN.
OO-AH, OO-AH.
ON THE FUNK TRAIN.
OO-AH, OO-AH.

WON'T YA CLIMB ON BOARD,
ALL YOUR FUNK WILL BE RESTORED,
ON THE FUNK TRAIN. FUNK TRAIN!

BUMP IT HIGH,
YOU CAN BUMP IT LOW,
YOU CAN BUMP YOUR THIGH,
BUMP YOUR LITTLE TOE.

BUMP, BUMP, BUMP YOUR BOOTY RUMP.
BUMP YOUR BOOTY RUMP!

REMEMBER THE GOOD TIMES WE HAD.
THE GOOD TIMES WERE BETTER, WERE BETTER THAN BAD.
THE BAD TIMES WILL JUST MAKE YOU SAD.
SO JUST REMEMBER THE GOOD TIMES,
JUST REMEMBER THE GOOD TIMES,
JUST REMEMBER THE GOOD TIMES,

AND WE'LL GO SYNCHRONISTIC DANCIN'

BARRY.

WE'LL SHOW YA HOW.

EVERYONE.

SYNCHRONISTIC DANCIN'

BARRY.

GET READY NOW.

EVERYONE.

WE'LL GO BALLISTIC DANCIN'
WE'LL DANCE OUR PANTS AWAY, AWAY, AWAY, AWAY!

BARRY. Thank you, Maple Valley!

(blackout)

End of Play

PROP & COSTUME LIST

ACT I

ONSTAGE

Furniture:

1 small table (24 inch by 24 inch – centerstage left)

4 stools (2 stage right and 2 stage left. Stage left stools, one is upstage of the table and one is downstage of the table)

Props and Dressing:

On the Table:

Four water bottles for the Synchronistics.

Downstage left:

A working telethon thermometer. As the pledges come in, the thermometer moves up to measure the progress. (See photo on website *www.PolyesterTheMusical.com*)

A black sheet over the thermometer to cover it at the beginning of the show.

On the Floor:

5 wireless microphones on mic stands. Depending on the size of the theatre, the microphones can be either working or just used as props. Four of the mics will be downstage center used by the four Synchronistics. The fifth microphone will be downstage left, next to the thermometer, used by Lance Chadwick, the host of the telethon.

On the back wall:

A big sign that reads:

"Maple Valley and the 1999
    WKLN TV Telethon
        Welcome
    The Synchronistics"

On a wall or hanging from the ceiling:

A working "On Air" sign.

Optional lighting:

Disco lights, i.e., a disco ball and other colorful flashing disco lights above the stage.

Lance brings in:

A VHS tape

A bicycle horn

A small disco ball on a string

A flashlight

Several note cards

Carl carries with him:

A ring box with no ring

Photos

ACT II

Lance brings in:

A Scotch glass with Scotch in it (preferably fake Scotch – Apple juice works well)

A coffee cup

Note cards

Carl brings in:

A neck brace

Barry carries with him:

A Visa credit card

COSTUMES

Colorful 70's disco costumes.

In the Los Angeles premiere, Lance Chadwick wore a polyester lime green tuxedo for both acts.

In the first act, the four Synchronistics wore white 70's costumes. The men wore John Travolta (*Saturday Night Fever*) style white polyester suits with white vests and black shirts. The women wore 70's style white mini-skirts with boots.

In the second act the women changed into colorful mini-skirts and boots, and the men wore colorful polyester shirts, and kept the white pants from the first act.

For photos of the costumes and the set from the Los Angeles premiere, visit *www.PolyesterTheMusical.com*

Telethon Thermometer

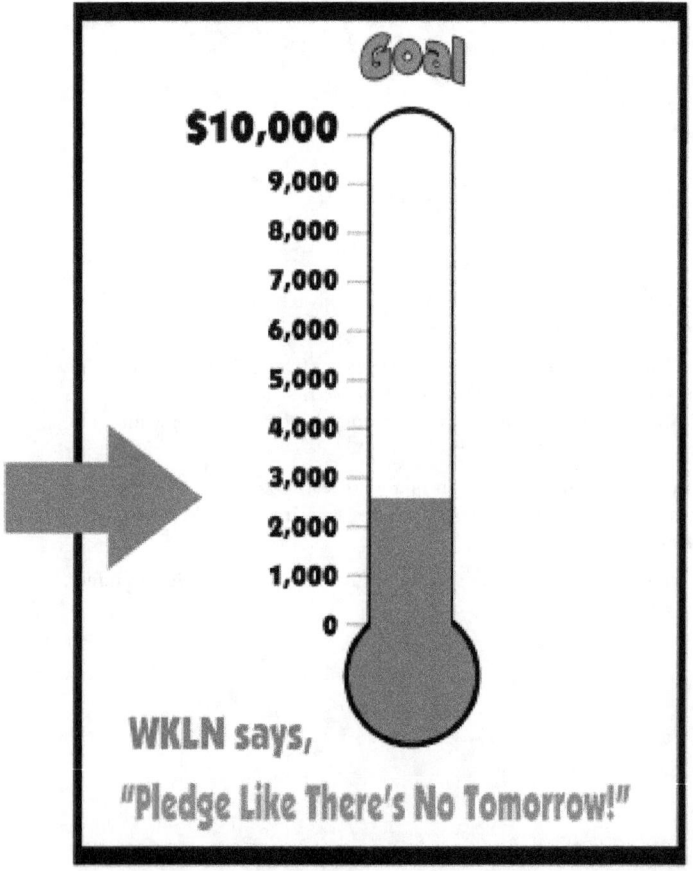

The Telethon Thermometer used in the Los Angeles premiere was 24 inches wide by 36 inches high, and rested on an easel. When a pledge came in, Lance would slide the arrow up, raising the "mercury" inside the thermometer toward the goal of $10,000.

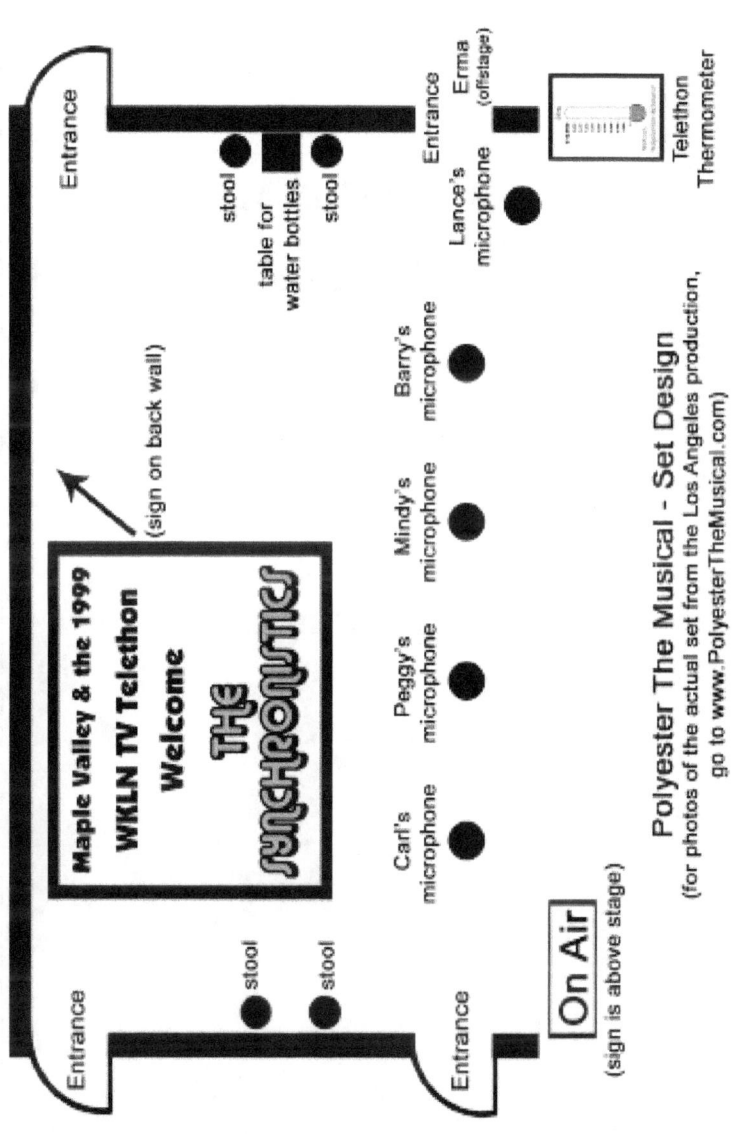

Polyester The Musical - Set Design
(for photos of the actual set from the Los Angeles production,
go to www.PolyesterTheMusical.com)

Also by
Phil Olson...

Don't Hug Me

A Don't Hug Me Christmas Carol

A Don't Hug Me County Fair

A Nice Family Gathering

Also by
Wayland Pickard...

eLove

Please visit our website **samuelfrench.com** for complete
descriptions and licensing information.

See what people are saying about
POLYESTER THE MUSICAL...

"I loved it!"
– Fred Willard

"Be sure to check out this toe-tapping, hilarious journey back to
your Dancing Queen days!...This show will take you back to the
70's, and you'll hardly be able to control your urge to get up on
stage and do "The Funk Train!""
– *Actors Entertainment*

"It's great fun!"
– *BroadwayWorld.com*

"A fun and entertaining evening with the audience moving and
grooving to the sounds of the 70's style original music and contagious
dancing in their seats. It's fun, fun, fun all the way through!...You will
have a ball! It's the perfect show to pick up your spirits!"
– *NoHoArtsDistrict.com*

"Audience members laughed uncontrollably throughout!..
Energetically entertaining!...A rollicking good time!"
– *The Tolucan Times*

"The 70's are back in *Polyester The Musical!* If you've ever wanted to
revisit the disco flash of the 70's, now's your chance!"
– *Musicals in LA*

"*Polyester The Musical* will become the next big thing!"
– *Accessibly Live - NoHo Arts*

"A fun-filled show!...Full of humor and the music and singing are
extremely entertaining!
– *Stage Happenings*

"I went to see *Polyester the Musical* with ten friends. Frankly, I was
annoyed that they laughed so loud that I missed some of the
dialogue and lyrics; until I discovered that I was one of the loudest
laughers. Go see it!"
– Ronald Jacobs, Producer/Director/Writer - *The Dick Van Dyke
Show, The Andy Griffith Show, That Girl, I Spy, The Mod Squad, Gomer
Pyle, Make Room For Daddy*

OTHER TITLES AVAILABLE FROM SAMUEL FRENCH

DON'T HUG ME

Book and Lyrics by Phil Olson
Music by Paul Olson

3m, 2f / Int.

It's *Fargo* meets *The Music Man* (without the blood or the trombones).

Oh, for cryin' in yer snow shoes! It's the coldest day of the year in Bunyan Bay when a slick karaoke salesman arrives at the bar and turns the locals' lives upside down. With its over the top songs and crazy characters, this "Minnesota love story with singin' and stuff" will have you laughing until the spring thaw!

Don't Hug Me takes place in Bunyan Bay, Minnesota. Cantankerous bar owner, Gunner Johnson, wants to sell the business and move to Florida. Clara, his wife and former Winter Carnival Bunyan Queen, wants to stay. Bernice Lundstrom, the pretty waitress, wants to pursue a singing career. Her fiance, Kanute Gunderson, wants her to stay home. It's a battle of wills, and when a fast-talking salesman, Aarvid Gisselsen, promises to bring romance into their lives through the 'magic' of karaoke, all heck breaks loose!

Featuring the songs, "I'm a Walleye Woman in a Crappie Town," "My Smorgasbord of Love," and "I Wanna Go to the Mall of America."

"A hokey jokey karaoke crowd pleaser!"
- Los Angeles Times

"A lot of laughs!...A great time! Go see it!"
- Tom Barnard, *KQRS*